STARCHILD AND WITCHFIRE

STARCHILD AND WITCHFIRE

David Henshall

For Emma, Lindsey, Little Oona,
for the real Jamie,
for Proberts,
for me,
and for L. J.
but, above all,
for HERSELF

First published 1990 by
MACMILLAN CHILDREN'S BOOKS
A division of Macmillan Publishers Limited
London and Basingstoke
Associated companies throughout the world

ISBN 0-333-53351-8

A CIP catalogue record for this book is available from the British Library

Typeset by Matrix, 21 Russell Street, London WC2
Printed by the Western Book Company Limited,

Contents

1

Snow

It was a blazing hot August morning and it was snowing like it sometimes does in the middle of winter. And, down below in the yard, there was a small Chilldrake patiently waiting to be acknowledged and let in so that he could carry out his mission. But, of course, Jamie Mercer hadn't seen the Chilldrake yet and, half asleep, he hadn't remembered that it was August. He simply lay in bed and thought nothing of the large flakes that swirled and gathered and danced at the window.

"Wonder if it's snowed enough to cover the boxes and bins in the corner," he thought sleepily.

To the left and right of number six Stubbs Terrace the old red-brick houses stood boarded up and decaying, waiting only for the local council to make up its mind as to who should be hired to pull them down. The small house where Jamie, his sister Fern and his mother lived was the only habitable one left in the whole row.

Jamie closed his eyes and wriggled deeper into the blankets. He peered at the battered alarm clock on the table at the side of his bed. It said five minutes past seven, and even though it had lost at least ten minutes in the night that still only made it a quarter past at the latest – and today was Saturday. He yawned loudly and tried to go back to sleep.

He'd almost made it too, when his bedroom door creaked open and Fern crept in. She stood for some moments and then said in a loud voice, "I know you're not asleep. I heard you yawning like a pig."

"Pigs don't yawn," Jamie replied. "They snore like you, fat-head." He turned over in bed and stared at Fern, who was standing with her thumb in her mouth.

"Take it out," Jamie said. "You're seven years old now and too big to suck your thumb. Only babies do that. No, on second thoughts, carry on. You are a baby."

"It's snowing, you know," Fern said.

"I know that," Jamie replied. "I saw it was as soon as I woke up. Now push off back to your own room."

Fern ignored him and sat down on the edge of his bed.

"I saw it was snowing first," she said. "I felt wide awake in the night and I opened the curtains and watched it through the window. I watched it for a long time. It just started out of nowhere and then it came on thick and fast just in our yard, and it's deep, deep, deep now. There's something else too," she added. "Only I don't think I'll tell you about it."

"And you're not going to let me get back to sleep either," Jamie said, poking an arm out for his dressing gown. "Do you fancy going sledging?" he asked, finding the garment and pulling it on.

Fern tutted. "In our yard?" she asked, pulling a face.

"No, you twit," said Jamie, jumping out of bed. "In the park. We'll get the sledge from under the stairs, and go before anybody else gets there."

"Dimmo," said Fern, using one of her favourite expressions. "There's only snow in *our* yard. I told you, only you don't listen. It fell for a long time, but there's none in the road and there's none on anybody else's roofs, only ours and in our yard, so there won't be any snow in the park, will there? And there's the thing out there as well," she added.

Jamie, not really listening, stood with his back to the clear white light that streamed in through the frosted windows.

"What thing?" he asked.

Fern closed her eyes and made her posh mouth. "Nething faw nowsey pawkers," she said.

"You snob," Jamie said.

"Pig!" Fern replied.

"Not everyone would trail about with a smelly sister," Jamie said. "And if you don't behave I won't take you anywhere."

"Don't care," said Fern, kneeling at the bottom of the bed to stare out of the window. "And you must be thick or something. I don't want to go anywhere, anyway. I want to stay in our yard where the snow is and keep cool. Yesterday was too hot. I'm going to stay and play with the lizard and build a snowman. I would have let it in last night but the window stuck and I couldn't get it open. I actually came in and tried to get you to do it but you wouldn't wake up."

"Please yourself," said Jamie, only half hearing. "I'll go sledging on my own." And then he stopped. But of course yesterday was hot. It had been a glorious August day. The snow that they were having now must be freak weather. Intrigued, he went to stand by Fern.

The snow lay deep, thick and deep and blue-white, with great flakes falling from the sky overhead, adding to the clean snow that covered the yard. He looked to the front and right and left, at the backs of the derelict and blind houses that made up three sides of the yard, and then he looked over their roofs and beyond to the streets and the roads that ran through that part of town.

The grubby streets were sun-washed and dusty in the early morning light, and a few people were up and about already, going into town in their shirt-sleeves or thin, cool dresses. Jamie looked back at the yard below the window, and at the thick snow that drifted and piled deeper even as he watched. He hated to admit it but Fern was right. The snow was only falling within the confines of the yard in Stubbs Terrace. And it wasn't falling from the sky either, but from somewhere just below the level of the rooftop. It was falling out of nothing, coming from nowhere.

Fern was sucking her thumb again but she suddenly snatched it out of her mouth and squealed.

"Oh, there it is. I thought it had gone. Yoo-oo. Come on, Lizzy, come up. Jamie, open the window, open the window and let it in. Please."

Jamie followed Fern's wave and saw what he took at first glance to be a large, white cat in the middle of the yard, hunched and spiky in the snow. And then he saw it look up, acknowledge Fern's wave with a squawk, a little steamy breath and a sudden flash of sapphire eyes. It spread a pair of large wings, gave an awkward hop and then swooped up to perch on the window-sill, staring in at them.

Fern laughed and tapped the window, as the creature rubbed its spiny back against the glass, leaving scratches where its diamond-hard backbone rubbed. Its deep blue eyes gazed first at Fern and then briefly at Jamie, and its white, marbled body and its wings, transparent and tipped with tiny claws, trembled with excitement.

"Let him in . . . Let the lizard in," Fern pleaded as the thing tapped urgently at the window with a glittering, metallic beak that looked sharp and hard enough to chip stone. On hearing Fern's voice the little creature became over-excited and scrabbled at the glass. Its diamond claws squealed down the pane like chalk down slate. It opened its beak and gave a "kark-kark" sound, loud and urgent.

Jamie, whether out of fear or sudden spite, suddenly snatched Fern from the bed, picked up a shoe and hurled it at the window as hard as he could. There was a crack and an interesting sound of smashed and tinkling glass that Fern would ordinarily have relished. Now, however, she simply screamed.

"You've killed it, you pig! You dimmo-pig! You've killed my Lizzie. I'll hate you for ever!"

She fought past Jamie, smacking out with her hands, and Jamie put both arms around her to hold her back.

"Mind the glass," he said, panicking now that he had broken the window. Fern only struggled harder.

"I'll get the glass and cut you to bits," she hissed through her teeth. And then she started to shout. "Mum! Mum!"

They were still locked together like that, with Fern yelling at the top of her voice, when their mother appeared in the doorway, red-faced, sleepy and extremely angry.

2

More Snow

Mrs Mercer was not pleased, either at being wakened so early or at the sight of the jagged hole in the window.

"It was an accident," said Jamie, still holding Fern, who had shut up and was looking at Mrs Mercer with an open mouth and wide eyes, waiting for the storm to break. Mrs Mercer clenched her fists so tightly that her knuckles went white and for a moment she looked as if she was going to scream. She looked at the children, huddled together on Jamie's bed, and then lowered her eyes, her body suddenly sagging into an attitude of utter weariness.

"Isn't it always?" said Mrs Mercer quietly. She seemed too weak and tired to stay angry. She dropped on to the bed and ran a hand through her straight, lank hair. "Was it really necessary?"

Jamie nodded and then shook his head and then nodded again, all in the space of a second, and then he pointed to the window.

"There's a lizard or something out there. It was trying to get inside. Fern wanted me to let it in. I wouldn't because it could be dangerous."

Mrs Mercer glanced at the window and then back at Jamie. She sighed, shaking her head.

"So you smashed it instead? Very intelligent, Jamie.

It's half past seven on a Saturday morning. I was cleaning at the Red Lion until gone midnight. I just want a bit of peace and quiet, and this is the sort of expensive stupidity that I can do without. I wish you two would act your age."

Jamie opened his mouth to say something. He hated to hear his mother talk like that. She never used to.

"It *was* there, Mum," Jamie persisted. "Fern saw it last night. I saw it this morning. A lizard or something like it. White with sharp claws. And there's snow. Snow in our yard and nowhere else." He looked to Fern for confirmation but Fern only glared back, sulky and tight-lipped.

Mrs Mercer pushed herself from the bed and made her way to the window, crunching shards of glass under her slippers. She stood in the yellow light and stared out.

"Snow," she said softly, her voice distant and sad. "There's no snow. There's no lizard."

Sunlight poured in and bathed the room in a warm glow.

"Get your clothes on and get out of the bedroom," said Mrs Mercer. "I won't bother with a lie-in today," she added, loud enough for the children to hear but quietly enough to make them think she was talking to herself. "I mean, who needs sleep?" She moved to the bedroom door and paused. "If the milk-lady knocks there's money in my red purse; pay her out of that. And don't forget to ask her to knock off the price of the pint that she didn't leave on Thursday."

Without even glancing behind her, Mrs Mercer closed the door and clumped off down the landing into her own bedroom to dress. Jamie stared at the window and then at Fern. How could their mother have failed to notice that the yard was full of snow while everywhere else was sweltering under a bright August morning sun?

Fern hopped on to the bed, looked out of the window and sniffed. She gave Jamie a withering, blaming kind of look and then ran off to the bathroom. Jamie got up and looked out.

The yard was empty, save for the rubbish that normally accumulated in all its corners. There were the boxes and the bins in the corner, the old bike and the cracked paving stones. There were the three old outside-toilets, one with the roof fallen in and the toilet pan smashed. There were the weeds, the junk and the dirt.

But there was no snow, and there was certainly no lizard, or whatever it was, perched on the window-sill. Jamie frowned.

"That's with you shouting. You made him go away. I hate you," said Fern, back from the bathroom, with toothpaste all over her face and not a great deal on her teeth. "You shouted like a crack-brain and you scared him off. You dimmo."

"You could have said something," Jamie argued, carefully picking up the bigger pieces of glass and dropping them into the yard. "You could have told Mum that you'd seen it too. Keeping quiet only made me look stupid. Mum probably thinks I was telling lies."

Fern shrugged, not caring, and Jamie started to get dressed, glancing from time to time at the window, hoping to see some stray flakes of impossible snow drift past the window.

"I think perhaps we dreamed it," said Jamie, talking slowly after a minute's thought. "Actually I don't mean dreamed. Miss Potter at school told us about this sort of thing once, where a lot of people stood in front of a statue of Jesus' mother and thought that they saw it move. She called it a Clective Loose Enation. It's when a lot of people think they see the same thing at the same time. That's what happened to us."

"I *did* see it," said Fern, unimpressed by anything that Miss Potter might have said. "I saw the snow, all of it, lots of it, in our yard, and there was none in any other yard, only in ours. And I saw the flying thing with the glass wings that sat on our window-sill. Course, it'd still be there only you had to go cracked and start throwing shoes. Anyway, you can see the lines down the window where its claws scraped. At least you could when there was a window there. So stuff Lucy Nation."

Jamie glared. "You carry on using language like that and I'll . . . "

"What? Tell Mum?" said Fern.

"Anyhow," Jamie went on, changing the subject. "Whoever heard of snow in August? Especially in one scruffy yard and nowhere else. Be sensible, Fern."

Fern laughed with as much sarcasm as all her seven years could muster. Jamie stood there with his arms out, just like Miss Potter.

"You're a dimmo," Fern muttered, unconvinced.

While Mrs Mercer was clearing away the broken glass, Fern and Jamie sat opposite each other at the rickety breakfast table in the middle room downstairs. They weren't speaking, but that had nothing to do with the mysterious snow and the equally strange lizard. While they had been getting their breakfasts Fern had reached into the fridge to get the last half-bottle of milk for the cornflakes. Jamie had jiggled Fern's arm and the milk bottle had fallen to the floor with a dull, wet smash. Jamie had said it was Fern's fault for not holding the bottle tight enough, and Fern had said it was Jamie's fault for being such a clumsy pig, with the result that neither of them would clean up the mess of milk and broken glass and there was no milk for the cornflakes until the milk-lady arrived.

Fern tried eating hers dry, but they all stuck to the roof of her mouth until she felt she was choking. Even spiting Jamie wasn't worth dying for, so she sat and played with the bowl until all the sugar trickled down through the cornflakes and settled at the bottom.

There was a knock at the door. Jamie narrowed his eyes and went to look for Mrs Mercer's red purse.

He had expected an argument but, apart from some low muttering, the milk-lady accepted the price of six pints just as Fern gave a loud cheer from somewhere in the house. Jamie smiled his thanks and then flew into the kitchen.

"I don't know if you think that's clever,' Jamie began angrily, and then he stopped as his foot hit something white and soft and slippery. He landed on his back in a soft snowdrift with the breath knocked out of him. He lay for a moment staring up at the kitchen ceiling, from which large white flakes drifted down. Fern's face loomed over him.

"He came back," said Fern with a wide grin and an excited light in her eyes. "He was scratching at the back door, so I let him in. Just look at all this snow." And then she added as an afterthought, "Have you broken a leg?"

Jamie sat up and grabbed a handful of cold, wet snow. He held it for a moment, stared at it, even rubbed a little of it against his cheek, before he let it fall. There was snow on the shelves, on the cooker, on the taps in the sink. It looked as if someone had left the back door open in a blizzard.

The little creature that was perched on Fern's right shoulder blinked its ice-blue eyes, and dug its claws a little deeper into Fern's shoulder, making her wince and wriggle. It was making small, happy noises in its throat.

"What's Mum going to say when she sees all this mess?" said Jamie, breathless with the shock of sliding into a kitchen full of cold snow.

"Not a lot . . . " said Mrs Mercer, who had just come down the stairs – and desperately felt like crying.

3

Something Really Strange

"Why not just take a hammer and smash everything?" said Mrs Mercer in a weary voice. "If you're going to do something then you might as well do it properly. Why is it always me that has to clear up after your messes?"

Jamie sat on the floor, his right knee an inch away from a jagged shard of the broken milk bottle. To Mrs Mercer it looked as if Jamie had skidded and fallen in the pool of milk that still lay on the uncarpeted floor. His foot had caught the rest of the broken glass and pushed it across the floor in one streak of white milk. Fern was staring about her and rubbing her shoulder as if she was looking for something. Mrs Mercer set down the brush and shovel that she was holding and lifted Jamie to his feet.

Jamie stared a question at Fern and Fern shrugged. Then he watched his mother clear away the mess in silence. Her silence always made him feel more guilty than her shouting. He opened the back door as his mother passed through to get to the bin in the corner of the yard.

"Where did it go?" he whispered to Fern. Fern shook her head and grinned.

"It isn't funny, you know," Jamie hissed. "First there's snow and then there isn't."

"I won't ask whose fault it was," said Mrs Mercer, returning from the yard. She filled the kettle and dropped one tea bag into a mug. Then, while she waited for the water to boil, she lit a cigarette and sat down in an armchair in the middle room. In her drab clothes Mrs Mercer blended well with the grey walls, the worn carpet and the dull light. The smoke from her cigarette curled in the air.

"I did see something really strange this morning, Mum," said Jamie brightly, as if repeating himself calmly and cheerfully would make his mother understand. The kettle in the kitchen clicked off the boil and Jamie filled the mug. "Something really, really strange at the window. And then, just now, there was something really strange in the kitchen. And I didn't just *see* it either. And it wasn't only me that saw it, was it, Fern? Fern saw it too, in fact Fern saw it first, because she woke up in the night and saw it then. Didn't you, Fern?'

Mrs Mercer took the tea that Jamie made and sipped it. Jamie could tell by the look in her eyes that she hadn't heard a word of what he'd said. Fern had the right idea. She had gone into the front room and was watching television. Nevertheless, Jamie felt it was important enough to make one last effort.

"Have you ever known it to snow in August, Mum?" he asked. Mrs Mercer seemed to revive as she pondered for a moment.

"I remember one bad winter," she said slowly. "I remember it very well because me and your Gran and your Grandad had just moved up from Manchester. Your Gran slipped on a patch of bad ice and had to spend that Christmas laid up in bed." Mrs Mercer paused and there was a slight, wistful expression in her eyes as if she was remembering something nice that had happened, not Gran's accident, all those years ago. Then she frowned. "That was a long time ago, long before I got married."

That final word came out with bitterness. It was the way she always spoke when she talked about anything to do with her husband. Jamie stood by the armchair, feeling awkward and ill at ease. He still remembered his father, even though there were no photographs of him in the house. Dad had never even written to say where or how he was, not even a card for birthdays or Christmas. It was as if he had decided that they were all unimportant. There was a knot in Jamie's stomach as he thought about his father. He was never bitter though, not like his mother.

A sudden sense of loyalty washed over Jamie. He and Fern were all Mrs Mercer had; even Gran and Grandad had died before Jamie was born. He wanted to go over and put his arms around her and hold her close. He wanted to tell her he loved her. All he said was: "Do you want another cup of tea?"

Mrs Mercer set down her mug and lit another cigarette. "I'll just have this, then I'll start tidying up," she said, trying a half-smile.

Jamie smiled back and went to look in on Fern. He paused at the door to the front room and half expected to see it full of snow and the lizard thing perched on Fern's shoulder. Fern was lying on the floor and she looked round when Jamie came in, mouthed the word "dimmo" and then turned back to the television. Jamie stalked over to where she lay and knelt down beside her.

"Listen, Fern," Jamie said. "You might think this is a big joke, but there's something weird happening and I don't like it. I don't like seeing things one minute and then not seeing them the next. It isn't right, no matter how much you grin like an ape. And I don't care how friendly you think that lizard might be, I still say it could be dangerous. It could be foreign, or escaped from a zoo, or have rabies or something. *And* I think it's got something to do with all the snow that comes and goes."

Fern looked up and rolled her eyes. "I should have thought that was obvious," she said. "Doesn't take brains to work that one out."

"Well, it isn't right," Jamie said. "I don't like it, and I'm going to get to the bottom of it."

Fern looked serious for one moment. "Well I *do* like it," she said. "It's the best thing that's happened around here for years, and I hope it happens again. I hope the Thing comes back as soon as it likes and stays for as long as it can. Only, next time it comes I shan't tell anyone. I'll just keep it all to myself. Everybody else just scares it away."

"I didn't scare it away the second time," Jamie said. "Mum did. It stayed in the kitchen while I was there. It only went when Mum came down."

"Huh," Fern said, not convinced. "Who threw the shoe?"

Jamie sat for a few minutes, thinking. He couldn't help but agree. Snow in August (and especially in the kitchen) was exciting, whichever way you looked at it. And the odd creature that made the snow, that was exciting too – and mysterious. He gazed around the room, almost willing the lizard to appear. He shut his eyes and tried to remember clearly what it had looked like.

It was white and had scales, rather like the small lizard that Fern thought it was. Its neck was long and its head was small and its strange, sparkling blue eyes, like a Siamese cat's only bigger and without pupils, seemed too large for its head. And then there were the wings, clear white wings like glass, except that they flapped and were flexible and more like polythene. And then there were the small claws that he felt must surely have left their mark in Fern's shoulder. Jamie stood up. Fixing the image of the creature in his mind had given him an idea.

"Fern, listen to me," he said, poking her with his foot.

Fern dragged her eyes away from the television.

"I'm going to go down into town. I know something special when I see it."

"What you going into town for?" said Fern, and then a sudden thought occurred to her. "You're not going to the police? They won't be interested. They'll lock you up for wasting their time."

"I'm not going to the police," said Jamie. "I want to go to the library and try and find out about that lizard. If I can find out exactly what it is then maybe we'll know how to deal with it if it comes back. *If* it shows up again, don't let on to Mum or anything. And if it doesn't come back then, then . . . well don't say anything either. Promise?"

Fern looked for one moment as if she was going to argue and then she changed her mind and nodded, turning back to the TV.

Jamie told his mother that he wouldn't be long and left the house. Miss Potter was always saying how useful the library was and now was probably the right time to take her advice. There were plenty of books in the library. Surely Jamie would find some answers there.

4

Mack

It was sweltering in the street, but Jamie didn't want to dawdle. There was no telling if, or when, the lizard thing would show again. He was red-faced and sweaty when he arrived. The young man behind the counter in the library was thin with bad spots on his face, and he was not very helpful. Jamie told him that he was doing a project at school on fabulous animals.

"You know, like dinosaurs, dragons and werewolves and – and Ewoks or something."

The young man shook his head and glanced nervously about him as if he was embarrassed to be seen talking to a young boy.

"Try Reference," he suggested, pointing vaguely to his right. "Through that door there. I think you probably want Heraldry."

Jamie nodded his thanks and pushed open the door that the young man had indicated. It was only a small library and the Reference section was no bigger than a large bedroom. There was a table with three chairs around it, one of which was occupied by an old man with white hair and sunglasses. He didn't look up when Jamie entered, but carried on running his long fingers over the pages of a book.

Jamie did three circuits of the small room, which

took him all of two minutes, but he really had no idea what sort of book he was looking for, so he found nothing.

The old man coughed and said, "Can I help you?"

Jamie pretended that he had not heard. He was facing away from the old man and he simply carried on looking along the shelves.

"I'm sorry," the old man persisted. "Excuse me, but can I help you? Are you looking for a particular book? I'm sure I can help you."

The old man pushed his own book away and stood up. Jamie caught a flash of white in the corner of his eye as the old man picked up a white stick, and he felt a little ashamed, realising that the old man was blind.

"Sorry," Jamie said hurriedly. "No, I don't think you can help, not really. I'm just looking, that's all."

The old man smiled and sat down. "And yet you came in here with such a purposeful step as if you knew exactly what it was you were looking for. I have an ear for such things." He cocked his head on one side and smiled. "Forgive me if I'm interfering. It's just that I have visited this place at least once a week for the past twenty years. In such a long time and in such a small building you tend to get to know where everything is, even if you can't see it."

"Heraldry, he said," Jamie blurted out quickly. "The man at the desk out there. It's for my project at school. We're doing monsters and things and he said that I should try Heraldry – only I don't know what that is."

The old man laughed. "Let me think now. Just give me a moment – yes. To your right there are five shelves. Third shelf, sixth or seventh book along. It should be quite a large one with, so I'm told, a brightly coloured spine. See it?"

Jamie looked; there was such a book. He pulled it down.

"*Boutell's Heraldry*!" he cried, and saw the old man bow in his chair as if he had just performed a conjuring trick. "Yes, thank you. I think this is what I want."

"It's very informative," said the old man. "A lot of people ask the assistants for it. That's why I know its place. Was there anything in particular that you wanted to look up? I only ask because heraldry was a hobby of mine when I was younger. I might be able to save you some time."

Jamie thought for a moment, casting a swift glance at the book on the table, the one that the old man had been holding when he had come in. Its pages were full of raised dots like pimples. The fact that the old man was blind made Jamie abandon a little of the usual shyness that he felt with people. He knew it was never a good idea to talk to strangers, but then again, they were in a public library, and the old man sounded well spoken and safe.

"Well," Jamie said, sitting at the table opposite the old man and opening the book at random, "it's like this. Miss Potter, she's our teacher, she did start to tell us a little bit about strange animals like, like" – he skimmed over some words on a page at random – "like a Torse and a Gooley – erm, I think it was a Gooley" – that sounded rude, Jamie thought – "but I forgot a lot of what she said and so I thought I'd better come and look them up." Jamie blushed suddenly.

The old man was laughing out loud. "If I remember right . . . " he said, finally composing himself, "a Torse is a kind of twisted ribbon. And Gule, which you so charmingly mispronounced – or is it misread? – is the heraldic term for the colour red. I don't think your Miss

Potter can have got her facts right if she suggested that they were the sort of fabulous animals the knights of old used to have in their coats of arms."

Jamie's blush deepened, but he couldn't confess why he really wanted to know about strange beasts. He felt silly enough as it was, without admitting to seeing flying lizards and snow where there shouldn't be snow. The old man held out a hand.

"McGee. First name Caspar, though no one has used it for forty years now, least of all me. People who get to know me generally call me Mack."

Jamie shook hands hesitantly. Mack's hand was cool and clean and his nails were well scrubbed and clipped at the ends of long, elegant fingers.

"Jamie," the boy said. "Jamie Mercer. Most of my friends call me Jim, and Fern calls me Dimmo because that's the new word at the moment, but I prefer Jamie."

"Quite right," Mack nodded. He bent his head forward as if he was looking at him through his dark glasses. "Did you really want to read about heraldry, Jamie?" he asked.

"Well," Jamie suddenly thought about Fern and what might be happening at home. "Yes, I did, sort of. But not for any project really. I made that bit up. Only, I can't say why I want to know." He paused and then decided to trust Mack, or partly trust him anyway. "Do you know what a creature might be called that's like a lizard, only bigger, about the size of a cat?"

"A salamander? Could that be it?" Mack suggested. "A long time ago it was thought that the salamanders lived in volcanoes. They are white, I think, but I can't pretend that they ever reached the size of a cat. Perhaps it's an axolotl you're thinking of; they're a bleached kind of white. They live under water as I recall. I can't really say how big they grow."

"Not those, I don't think," said Jamie. "This thing has wings too and clawed feet, and the wings are see-through, like plastic, only of course it can flap them and use them to fly."

Mack's forehead crinkled as he frowned behind his glasses. "Might it be some sort of dragon perhaps?" he said, in an odd voice.

"That's what I was wondering," Jamie agreed, not noticing the change in Mack's tone. "But dragons, at least all the dragons that I've ever read about, breathe fire and smoke and are quite large. This thing is small, I mean I thought that it was a cat at first, that's about how big it is, and Fern thought it was a lizard, but I'm not so sure because – because of the wings. It *might* be a dragon, but then it breathes snow. That is, a lot of snow starts falling whenever it's around."

Mack was quiet and serious. When Jamie said that the lizard breathed snow, he had given a small start.

"What you saw was a Chilldrake," Mack said slowly. "But you wouldn't have found it in any heraldry book. In fact you wouldn't have found any mention of it in any book in this place. That's what it is though."

"A Chilldrake?" Jamie repeated. The chill part was obvious, but he had always thought that a drake was some sort of duck. He said as much and Mack smiled.

"A wurm is the mediaeval term for a dragon. Sometimes people referred to them as drakes, though strictly speaking the drakes were the dragons without wings, the ones that could only crawl. The Firewurms were the larger, the more dangerous ones that breathed flames. They were also the ones that flew. Any decent bestiary will tell you as much. But Chilldrakes, now they're quite another thing. They are related to the big dragons, much the same way that a cat is related to a lion, hence the term 'drakes'. 'Chill', obviously because the particular little creatures that you describe breathe out cold and generally create their own small winters wherever they go." Mack paused to let all this information sink in and muttered, "But it's quite extraordinary to hear someone ask about *them*, and after all this time, too . . . "

Jamie stared at Mack's eyes, or rather he stared at the reflection of his own face in the black lenses of Mack's dark glasses.

"A Chilldrake, yes, that's what it is, Mack. I mean, I don't know how you know all this if it isn't in any book but that's what it is. It made snow in our back yard last night and this morning. It even tried to get into the house. And downstairs, while it was perched on Fern's shoulder, it made snow in the kitchen, only when Mum appeared the Chilldrake and the snow just went, vanished. And it's probably making snow right now all over our front room while Fern's watching the television. Do you think I'm mad? Fern saw it too, I swear she did, only it sounds so stupid."

Jamie stopped and waited for Mack to laugh. Mack stayed quiet and serious, tapping the floor with the tip of his stick; then he closed his book.

"I don't think you're mad," he said, smiling in a friendly way. "Not mad at all. And, before you ask, I don't think you and your sister were dreaming either." Mack leaned forward and made a pretence of looking round with his blind eyes to see if anyone was listening. "Though, if seeing a Chilldrake makes you mad, then I must be too, because I've seen one."

"You have?" Jamie asked suspiciously.

"I haven't always been blind, you know, and yes, I

have seen a Chilldrake. In fact, it was almost certainly the same one that caused its little havoc at your house this morning."

Jamie still couldn't be sure that Mack was telling the truth or if he was joining in some sort of fantasy game that he thought Jamie was playing.

"What colour are their eyes?" he asked, trying to sound casual.

"Ah, I see," Mack said. "This is to test if I'm telling the truth or just stringing you along for the fun of it? Chilldrakes' eyes are blue, Jamie Mercer, blue as the deep blue fires of winter, blue as the blood of a sapphire. Do I pass the test? Do you believe me now?"

"Yes," said Jamie, sure of Mack's honesty now. "*Are* they dangerous? I thought that its claws looked deadly."

Mack's serious expression melted and he smiled for a brief moment.

"Not dangerous, Jamie, not in themselves." Mack rubbed his chin. "But that's not to say that they are *safe*. In fact, it's probably true to say that, right at this moment, your house is just about the most *unsafe* place anyone could wish to be . . . "

5

Miss Dummel

There was a knock at the door at the small house in Stubbs Terrace. Fern waited for a moment for her mother to open the door but she didn't appear. When the knock sounded again Fern went to see who it was. She stood on one leg and stared at the person who was keeping her from the episode of *Buzz Beddows and the Stargang*, which was still playing loudly on the television behind her.

"Is your daddy in?" said a large fat woman in a pink coat that came down to her ankles. She had a clipboard under her arm and a pen in her hand that had a small plastic gargoyle stuck on the end of it. Fern had always wanted one of those and it held her attention for some moments until the fat woman said again, "Is your daddy in?"

Fern shook her head, unwilling to tell a total stranger that she hadn't seen her father for years. Fern turned her head slightly to catch a sight of Revoltron, the renegade robot of the planet Znarl, ordering a death sentence on Buzz Beddows, the handsome captain of the starship *Astrogon* and leader of the Stargang, defenders of the Earth against its enemies. The large woman in pink spoke for a third time. There was an irritable edge to her voice, as if she had better things to do and Fern was keeping her from doing them.

"Well, can I speak to your mummy then?"

Fern sighed and went into the middle room, where Mrs Mercer was dozing in the chair. Fern took the cigarette stub that had burned down between her mother's fingers and shook her shoulder.

"Mum," she said in a loud voice that the sound of the television fortunately drowned. "There's a fat woman at the door."

"What?" said Mrs Mercer, coming awake. "Who is she? What does she want?"

"Hello-oh," warbled the woman at the door. "Mrs Mercer, isn't it? I'm sorry to bother you, but I shan't keep you long. Just a moment, that's all. Can I come in?" And, without waiting for an answer, the large woman stepped inside the house and closed the door behind her.

Mrs Mercer smoothed down her hair and cast a hurried glance at herself in the mirror over the fireplace. She tutted, not much liking what she saw. "Why did you let her in?" she whispered to Fern, who had no time to reply before her mother went into the front room and turned off Revoltron and the Stargang.

Fern followed her mother and stared at the woman who was depriving her of the sight of Buzz as he was about to snare the renegade robot from the plant Znarl in the *Astrogon*'s energy net, from which there was never any escape, no matter how much Revoltron blasted and struggled.

"Is it about the electricity bill?" Mrs Mercer asked, with a note of alarm in her voice. "Only I did write to your people and tell you how things are at the moment. I will pay everything I owe, only— "

"Heavens, no," said the large woman, opening her red-lipsticked mouth in a wide smile. "I'm Miss Dummel, from the Truepoll Research Agency. There's my card, see . . . Dummel, Truepoll. Just here to ask a few questions."

Mrs Mercer looked both relieved that the woman wasn't there for money and a little apprehensive about being asked questions. Fern listened to Miss Dummel's rolling, plummy accent and made a face.

"Well, I don't know . . . " Mrs Mercer began. Miss Dummel threw her large self into an armchair.

"I know how busy you must be," she panted. "And we appreciate that at Truepoll." As she spoke, Miss Dummel drew a small envelope from the papers on her clipboard. "Fifteen pounds, just for your time and trouble. Cash."

Mrs Mercer held out her hand and Miss Dummel drew back the envelope quickly. "If I could just have a few minutes of your time?"

Mrs Mercer nodded reluctantly and Miss Dummel settled herself with difficulty deeper into the armchair. Fern stood by the middle door. Miss Dummel was quite old, Fern decided, at least thirty and she smelled of scent and talcum powder and soap. Hers was a perfume that hung in the air about her like a cloud and seemed to make the stale smell of the parlour of Stubbs Terrace all the stronger in comparison.

"What a lovely daughter you have," Miss Dummel beamed, staring at Fern, who was scowling and wrinkling her nose in an unlovely way. "Do you have any other children?"

"There's Jamie," Mrs Mercer replied, and she watched as Miss Dummel put a tick on one of the sheets on her clipboard. "He's older. He's . . . Where is Jim, Fern?"

"Library," said Fern. "Can I watch the Stargang? It's at a good bit."

"Oh, we won't be long, dear," Miss Dummel said quickly. "Just want to ask your mummy a few simple questions and then you can all get back to doing whatever it was you were doing. There's a good girl."

Miss Dummel had a sing-song voice that Fern decided was supposed to sound friendly and make people like her. Fern also decided, from the way that Miss Dummel curled her nostrils and the way that she cast tiny glances at the unvacuumed carpet, that this was the last place Miss Dummel wanted to be on a fine Saturday morning.

"What sort of dishwasher do you have, dear?" Miss Dummel asked suddenly, smiling her large grin at Mrs Mercer. Mrs Mercer stammered a little and said she didn't have one, whereupon Miss Dummel, with a sniff, put a dark cross somewhere on her clipboard.

Fern listened for a while and then got bored with standing and sat down on the settee, as far away from the sweet-scented fat Miss Dummel as she could get without leaving the room. What daft questions the woman was asking, Fern thought. Fancy asking her mother what make of car she drove. Didn't the silly woman know where she was? Couldn't she see that they didn't have a Ninfer Red See Dee, whatever that was, or Cavity-wall Insulation?

Fern listened to her mother, trying as best she could to answer all Miss Dummel's ridiculous questions.

"Oh no, we don't have an automatic washer. I wouldn't mind one though, what with my two." And then Miss Dummel asked another question which Fern couldn't quite catch but which made her mother shift uncomfortably in her chair.

Fern felt suddenly angry, and she didn't know why.

Her mother sounded almost *ashamed* that she couldn't answer the questions with the answers that Miss Dummel was obviously looking for. Fat and pongy Miss Dummel, with her pink coat and her clipboard and pen with the plastic gargoyle that bobbed its head as she wrote. Fern felt that Miss Dummel would probably laugh about them when she left the house. Yes, well, Fern would give the fat woman something that she couldn't laugh about.

"We've got a snow-lizard!" she blurted out and Miss Dummel paused in mid sentence, her ball-point hovering over the paper.

"Sorry, chick, what was that?" Miss Dummel asked, a slight frown on her face. Fern tried to outstare Miss Dummel but her eyes wavered. "I said we've got a snow-lizard," she repeated more quietly. "And I bet there isn't a house that you've been in today that's got one."

Mrs Mercer shrugged her shoulders and attempted a smile. "Fern, love," she said. "Why don't you— "

"It's true!" Fern cried, seeing the smile disappear from Miss Dummel's face. "We haven't got a dishwasher and doovays, and we haven't got a car. And we might not have a dad neither, just in case you were thinking of asking, but we've got a snow-lizard and that's better than anything. Better than being in the Stargang."

Miss Dummel's grin reappeared and her teeth showed white, like square Mint Imperials, through her red lips. "What's a snow-lizard, dear? Is it some kind of pet?" she asked, staring straight at Fern and letting her clipboard droop.

Fern looked at her mother.

"You know what children are like. They say anything to get attention," Mrs Mercer said. "Are we nearly finished now?"

Miss Dummel brought her eyes away from Fern with what seemed to be an effort. "What?" she said abruptly, and then, "Sorry? Oh, yes, nearly finished, and then I can give you your envelope, Mrs Mercer." Miss Dummel turned again to Fern and her eyes narrowed until they were slits in her powdered face. "Just the one last question."

She made a pretence of checking her clipboard. "Oh, yes, and I see that this one is for the little girl, for Fern." Miss Dummel's smile went fixed upon her face as if it had been glued there. "What a strange name. Fern. I always think of ferns as being a sort of weed. Still, I expect you knew what you were doing when you picked it."

Mrs Mercer frowned. "I beg your pardon?" she said, rallying a little of the temper that had lately been reserved for her children.

Miss Dummel waved her quiet with one fat hand. "I said I had just the one question and then you can have your money and I'll be away. Providing, that is, that your kid gives the right answer," she said, and all the sing-song had died out of her voice to be replaced by something hard and harsh and unpleasant. "Where *is* your little snow-lizard? You see, I know it has been here. It's really what I came for."

Fern was silent. Mrs Mercer was silent, surprised by the abrupt change in Miss Dummel's manner. Fern opened her mouth to speak and then closed it, firmly.

Miss Dummel stood up with an effort. "I'll ask again, in words you can understand," she said. "Where is the Chilldrake, you little brat?"

Mrs Mercer stood. "Now you just see here— " she began and then stopped.

Miss Dummel seemed to be getting taller in front

of them, and there was an odd glint in her eyes. The clipboard clattered to the floor and the plastic gargoyle fell off the end of Miss Dummel's pen.

Fern had seen many strange things on television, and she had read equally strange things in her role-playing books, but never anything quite like what she was seeing now. Her mouth fell open as Miss Dummel took a deep breath and began to stretch, slowly and surely, as if she was a rubber-band being pulled by invisible fingers. Her whole body was drawn out, long and thin, all her fat taking up the slack of her transformation until she stood tall and terrible with her hair brushing the parlour ceiling and the hem of the pink coat now above her knees. Miss Dummel's face started to change too, turning from a plump, powdered and painted attempt at niceness into a dry, wrinkled and hideous old face with staring and sunken eyes, framed by grey and straggling hair. If she stretched out any more, Fern thought, she would poke up into her mother's bedroom above.

"*Where is the Childrake*!" the new Miss Dummel bellowed, her voice cracked and harsh and her thin red lips curled in a snarl. "I can smell the traces of it. I know it has been here and I shall not leave empty-handed. And, if need be . . . " she added, swiping a bony hand in an arc through the air, "I shall tear down this stinking hovel to find it. The pretence is over! I want what I came for!"

Mrs Mercer, unsure and panicking, reached for the poker from the hearth. Fern hid her face and screamed, and didn't see the bolt of white fire that snaked from Miss Dummel's eyes. It sizzled around Mrs Mercer and she fell back into her chair. Hearing the poker clatter Fern screamed again. Miss Dummel had sounded just like Revoltron, the renegade robot from the planet

Znarl. Fern curled up into the corner of the settee as Miss Dummel's now large and clawed hand reached out towards her.

"Oh God, oh God, oh God," Fern thought, hearing the hiss of Miss Dummel's laboured breathing. "What would Buzz Beddows do now . . . ?"

6

Karrax for Short

Mack sat at the table in the Reference room of the library and drummed his fingers on the scratched wood for a long time. Jamie, worried by what Mack had said about the Chilldrake not being safe, sat at the opposite end and waited. The old man had believed everything he had heard and Jamie wasn't at all surprised when Mack finally broke the silence and suggested that they both go back to Stubbs Terrace, if only to make sure that the Chilldrake had not reappeared.

"The house won't be very tidy," Jamie said, taking Mack's hand. "Mum doesn't bother much with housework. She used to, but since Dad left having a tidy house doesn't seem to matter, not to Mum anyway. She's too busy, you see— ' He stopped suddenly, just as they passed through the door of the Reference room into the main body of the library. The air seemed to waver in front of him, like air sometimes does on a very hot summer's day, and the whole of the library beyond shimmered and wavered. The spotty young man looked up for a second and frowned and then his image curled and crinkled and shook alarmingly, all his features running like smoke.

Jamie clung to the door handle. He felt as if he was being pulled away and lifted into the air by a great wind. For a second he almost lost his grip. And then everything righted itself just as suddenly. The young man was still frowning after them as they left, though he seemed to have noticed nothing.

"What happened?" Jamie asked.

"I can't explain right now," said Mack quietly. "But I think we had better hurry."

The town streets were crowded, but Mack wove his way in and out of the bustle, avoiding the old ladies with bags who walked two abreast, gossiping. He dodged the young mothers with their prams wedged in shop doorways, tapping along with his stick quickly and surely until they came to the traffic lights at the end of the main road.

"I am not sure of the way from here," Mack said. "It's a part of town I'm not familiar with. You will have to lead, Jamie."

They crossed the road and made their way past rows of shops that became shabbier and less well stocked. The day was hotter now, but there was a closeness in the air, a stickiness that made walking unpleasant. Jamie could feel his shirt clinging to his back, though Mack seemed unruffled by the heat.

"It's not far now," Jamie said. "Our street is just past the newsagents on the left."

Mack nodded. There was a grim look on his face. Jamie wondered what his mother would say when he appeared at the door with an elderly blind man with white hair.

They turned into Stubbs Terrace just as a large woman in a long pink coat came round the corner. She paused, and stared at Jamie and Mack briefly with such an expression of frustrated anger that it made Jamie flinch, and then she scowled and barged past them, knocking Mack to one side. Mack steadied himself and then sniffed the air. A heady odour of strong scent and fancy soap wafted along the street.

"Who was that?" he asked Jamie. Jamie stared after the rude fat woman as she crossed the main road in a flurry of pink. Her shape shimmered like a heat-wave.

"Some woman," Jamie said. "I've never seen her before, but whoever she is she has no manners. She didn't even apologise. Here we are, Mack."

Jamie laid his hand on the flaking black paint of the front door and pushed. The door didn't move. "Fern must've locked the door after me," he said, knocking loudly. Jamie and Mack waited a moment, then Jamie knocked again. From the other side of the door Fern's voice called out, small and frightened. "Who is it?"

"It's me, Ferny," Jamie said.

"How do I know it's you?" Fern called. "You could be anybody. You could be the witch come back in Jamie's body. Prove it's you."

Jamie looked at Mack and frowned apologetically. "She's silly like that sometimes. Fern! Fern, open the door, now!"

There was a long silence and then the letter-box in the centre of the door opened slowly and two eyes peered out. Then the eyes disappeared and Fern's mouth appeared at the opening.

"Who's the tall old man with you?"

"It's Mack – Mr McGee – we met in the library." Then Jamie dropped his voice to a whisper. "And don't be so rude. He knows all about what we saw this morning."

"You've told!" Fern's lips said through the letter-box. "You made *me* promise not to tell and you've gone blabbing it to everybody, you big mouth. I expect you told Smelly Dummel too." Fern unlocked the door and threw it open with a bang. "Oh, and Mum's fainted."

Jamie rushed in, followed by Mack. Mrs Mercer was slumped in the chair and wouldn't wake up, not even when Jamie shook her hard. "What happened, Fern?" he asked.

Fern was gazing at Mack's dark glasses and his cane. "There was this woman and she was asking all sorts of stupid questions about washing machines and things," she said, not taking her eyes from Mack. "And I got fed up with her because she was making Mum embarrassed, so I told her that we'd got a snow-lizard and then she got rude and called me a brat and a weed and said she was going to pull the house down. She called the snow-lizard a cold duck or something and kept asking me where it was, and when I wouldn't tell her, because I couldn't, she got all stretched and her head hit the ceiling. Then Mum fainted. I scrunched up on the sofa and screamed. And that's when Lizzy came back, just like that. He saw the fat woman, only she was all tall and ugly now, and she made a grab at Lizzy, but he flew towards the front door and vanished. So she went fat again like a rubber-band when you let it go. And then she left just before you got here." Fern paused for a breath and added: "Are you blind, Mr Magoo?"

Mack felt his way over to the chair where Mrs Mercer had slumped. He took her wrist and felt her pulse and then placed his cool hand on her brow, arranging his long fingers in a strange pattern and pressing them lightly at Mrs Mercer's temples.

"Is she all right, Mack?" Jamie asked, and Mack nodded, withdrawing his hand. "She'll be fine, but I don't think we ought to wake her. I should let her sleep." He turned to Fern. "And what about you, Fern? Were you very frightened by this strange woman?"

"Um, a little bit," Fern replied. "But I kept thinking what Buzz Beddows would do. He's the leader of the Stargang, you know, and the bravest man alive. He'd splatter one fat woman in a pink mac no matter how much she turned nasty, only – only I didn't need to do anything because she cleared off. Ow!"

Fern's sudden cry was because of the small sharp pain in her shoulder and the soft cold of snowflakes on her face.

"It's the Chilldrake, Mack," Jamie breathed, seeing the little snow-dragon again. "It's come back. It's on Fern's shoulder."

The Chilldrake rubbed its tiny head against Fern's cheek.

"He's purring!" Fern said, brushing the snow from her nose. "This is wonderful! Don't you dare start shouting, Jamie. You'll scare him off, or you'll wake Mum and the same thing will happen."

Jamie sat by his mother, his hand on hers. He watched the large white flakes of snow fall from the ceiling. It *was* extraordinarily beautiful, the way the snow appeared from nowhere. Jamie looked at the small Chilldrake on Fern's shoulder and the smallest twinge of the fear and jealousy that had made him throw the shoe that morning gripped him for a second. Mack clicked his fingers and the Chilldrake took wing and flapped on to Mack's forearm. Its large blue eyes sparkled as if there was a light behind them.

"Is he yours, Mr Magoo?" Fern asked, half-afraid that Mack would say it was and take it away.

"He belongs to no one," Mack replied, stroking the Chilldrake's head with one finger. "Though I think he must have taken a fancy to you, Fern."

Fern grinned. "I saw him first, first before anyone,

before Jamie anyway. Does he have a name? I mean, a proper name? I call him Lizzy, but I don't suppose it really is that." Fern readily accepted that Mack knew everything that there was to know about Chilldrakes.

"He has a very long name. It's *Koarinaximoradwior-atinnarion-illioth*, and that's just what you might call his Christian name. But he answers to Karrax, thankfully," Mack said, and he shook his white hair free of the snow that had settled there. The snow covered the threadbare settee and chairs and piled into small drifts on the mantelpiece. "He also gets a little carried away when he's happy or excited. *Cadoar mae ferrinan, Koarinax.* May we have the snow *off*, please?"

The Chilldrake whirred in its throat and flapped its clear wings. Instantly the snow was gone, and only the cold feel of it lingered in the air of the parlour. The front room seemed more seedy than ever, with only the little jewel of the Chilldrake itself at all special there.

"How do you know so much about him, Mr Magoo?" Fern asked, putting into words the question that was hovering at the back of Jamie's mind. "And do you know that fat woman too? *She* knew that the Chilldrake was here. She said she could smell it. She'd come looking for it, only she didn't say why."

"I think," said Mack quietly, "I think that there's a lot of explaining to be done. I owe you that much at least. Is there somewhere we can go to talk? I'd rather we left your mother sleeping a little while longer. The sight of me and this fellow, beautiful as he is, might just prove more than she could take." Mack's voice fell to a confidential whisper. "You know what adults are like."

"But what's wrong with Mum?" Jamie asked worriedly. "Is she unconscious because of something that woman did to her? Shouldn't we get a doctor?"

Mack shook his head. "I rather think your mother simply fainted," Mack said. "If I read the matter right, then your mother has just seen a dangerous woman called Malvolia Du Mal reveal the darker side of herself. The dumpy shape and the pink coat is the way she normally moves around, but she has the ability, as Fern and your mother saw, to become someone – or rather, something – quite different."

"Then that was her!" Jamie cried. "That was the woman who barged into us at the end of the road."

"Yes," Mack agreed. "I recognised her scent. Seeing Malvolia change as she did would have been enough to frighten anyone into fainting. Anyone except you, Fern, of course. You're clearly made of stronger stuff than that."

Fern beamed. No one had ever paid her so many compliments before.

"When I touched your mother's forehead I sent her into a deep and forgetful sleep. She's resting now and, when she does wake, she'll remember nothing. You've trusted me enough already, Jamie, but after I've explained matters, perhaps you'll trust me all the more."

"There's the middle room," Jamie said. Fern took Mack's hand and led him out of the parlour. In the middle room the Chilldrake flew to the top of the mirror over the fireplace, where he perched and looked at himself upside-down in the dusty glass. The mirror frosted over wherever the Chilldrake breathed upon it. Karrax seemed content to sit there waiting as Jamie and Fern settled down to hear what Mack had to tell. As Mack began, Mrs Mercer, peaceful in the parlour, smiled in her sleep and dreamed of another snowy summer long ago.

7

Mack Explains

"Before we met in the library this morning, Jamie," Mack said, "I had no idea that any of this would happen. The last thing in the world I imagined was that an enterprising young chap" – here Jamie flushed despite himself – "would march in and start looking for information about Chilldrakes. It takes a lot to shock a body as old as me, but I *was* shocked, I can tell you. Chilldrakes are rare and shy things, they seldom wander far from their own homes and, since only a handful of people know of their existence, I was – well – apprehensive about telling you anything. And then I realised that you must have actually seen one to be able to describe it so well. I told you, Jamie, that Chilldrakes aren't safe. I hope I didn't give you the wrong impression. There's not a trace of malice in them, or anything like that. It's just that – how can I put it? – things seem to happen when that little fellow appears. When we left the library and you experienced that dragging feeling – yes, I could sense it too – then I knew there was something wrong. I have felt that slipping sensation too many times to think that it was anything other than Malvolia Du Mal at work somewhere nearby. Not many know when she's about. In fact, Jamie, you only felt what you did because you were close to me at the time."

Fern was listening patiently enough, and following as best she could. "Are you a wizard, Mr Magoo?" she asked.

Mack smiled. "I think you can call me Mack. All my friends do. And, yes, I suppose you could call me a wizard, though don't expect me to do any tricks or anything like that. Malvolia is the one for tricks. Only her sort of magic happens to be of the worst kind."

"Where do Chilldrakes come from?" Jamie asked. "Do they live at the North Pole or somewhere like that?"

Mack frowned. "Not exactly."

"Another planet!" said Fern, with a vague recollection of seeing Buzz Beddows tackle something similar. "Do they have spaceships like the *Astrogon*?"

Mack laughed. "They're not aliens, Fern, though in a sense you're close enough to the truth. They certainly do come from a world very different from this one, but it's a world that's nearer than you might think."

"What's it called, their world?" asked Fern.

Mack thought for a moment. "It has had many names in the past," he replied, "but we'll call it Mithaca. It's pretty much how the people there refer to it."

"Mithaca," Fern said, liking the sound of the word. "And what about Mal . . . Malwhatyousaid?" she asked. "Is she from there too? She told lies and she said her name was Dummel, and she stinked – stunk. She smelled like a whole make-up counter. And why does she want Karrax?"

At the sound of his name the Chilldrake looked up and spread his wings, and flew to the back of the chair where Jamie and Fern sat. They could feel his breath like an icy draught on the back of their necks. Jamie thought that Mack suddenly looked a little sad.

"Malvolia Du Mal from Mithaca? Gracious no, she's not from Mithaca. Though she would like to get there. And, if she ever laid her hands on Karrax, she would too, without any problem. Karrax is quite extraordinary, even for a Chilldrake. He's a skipper, you see, and probably unique. He can travel – I like to think of it as skipping because he does it so fast – from Mithaca to here and back again. And the thing is, he can take others with him too. Malvolia sees Karrax as the way she can enter Mithaca. Not that Karrax would take her willingly, of course, but if she ever did persuade him to take her to Mithaca . . . well, it would be like, like throwing a cat into an aviary. Malvolia wants power and she wants to rule, and she doesn't have enough clout or enough followers mindless enough to help her do that in this world."

Jamie frowned. Stories of creatures skipping between this world and another were hard to believe, although Mack seemed serious, and Jamie himself had seen the Chilldrake. He decided to give Mack the benefit of the doubt, for a while at least.

"But why is Karrax here at all?" he asked. "I mean, if Malvolia can sense him, then his being here, in this world, puts Mithaca in the worst possible danger. Doesn't he have the sense to realise that?"

"It has to be something very important to make him keep coming here," Mack agreed.

Jamie stared around at their untidy, ill-kept little house. He couldn't imagine anything there interesting enough to make the Chilldrake appear even once.

"What else is there in Mithaca?" Fern said. "I mean, it isn't just full of Chilldrakes, is it?"

"No, Fern," said Mack, and Jamie thought that he looked glad of the slight change of topic. "Think of Mithaca as another world completely. Much of it is commonplace and ordinary, but, just as there are rare and strange things in this world, so too in Mithaca there are wonderful and different creatures like Karrax. He took me there, you know, just the once, to let me see his home."

"I wish he would take me," Fern sighed. "Sarah Mellor at school, she's been to Disneyland, but I bet Mithaca is better."

"No doubt," Mack agreed. "And it is far more dangerous too. They aren't all friendly like Karrax, you know. There are terrible things in that world, just as there are in this." Mack shivered as if he was remembering something painful. "It was while I was there that I went blind," he said, and then fell silent.

"Would you like a cup of tea?" Jamie asked to break the silence. "It's no trouble."

Mack's friendly smile returned to his old face. "I would love one," he said. "Milk and no sugar, please."

Jamie went into the kitchen and filled the kettle. The noise of the water splashing from the tap covered the sound of the rush of wings and he winced at the pricking in his shoulder as Karrax landed there. He felt the goose-bumps rise as Karrax blew little icy breaths into his ear.

"Don't," Jamie whispered, stroking the Chilldrake along its cold throat. "I might get chilblains."

Karrax thrummed like a big tabby. Now that Jamie could examine him closely, he saw that Karrax's eyes were made up of tiny hexagons, like the eyes of a dragonfly. They looked like turquoise gems.

Jamie switched on the kettle, rummaged through the dishes in the sink and chose an unchipped mug, swishing it out under the tap until it was clean enough. From the middle room came the sounds of Fern and Mack still talking.

Jamie waited for the kettle to boil and stared out of the window at the yard.

"Why *did* you come here, Karrax?" he said, wondering how intelligent the little dragon was and if it could understand him at all. "Why here to this dumpy old yard in this dumpy old town?"

Karrax made a soft noise that sounded like "kark-kark".

"Fern was right, you know, Karrax," Jamie whispered. "You are the best thing that has ever happened to us. You're certainly the most beautiful thing that I've ever seen." Then he thought to himself, with a sinking feeling, "And I could never tell anyone about you because they wouldn't believe me." He went and stood in the doorway to the middle room, squirming at the talons that dug into his shoulder as the little dragon maintained its balance.

"Tea won't be long," Jamie said.

"I'll have milk and a chocolate biscuit. No, I'll have two," said Fern, taking advantage of the occasion. It wasn't every day that a wizard had tea with her.

"What'll happen now, Mack?" Jamie asked. "I mean, how long do you think Karrax will stay around?"

Mack spread his hands. "I really don't know," he admitted.

"Will you always be our friend, even when Karrax isn't here, Mr Mack?" said Fern.

Mack laughed. "How could we not stay friends, when we have a Chilldrake in common?"

Jamie felt oddly happy. The Chilldrake on his shoulder, the fact that he was making tea for a wizard, even the creepy, stretching Miss Dummel; it all seemed quite natural. He peeped in on his mother, who was still sleeping with a smile on her face, and then returned to the kitchen as the kettle boiled. He made the tea and was just about to get Fern's biscuits when Karrax started to hum. It wasn't the pleased, purring whirr that he had made when Jamie stroked him – this was more of a growling. At first Jamie thought the heat from the steam of the boiling kettle had upset the Chilldrake, but then he caught a sudden glimpse of pink at the window.

"It's the fat woman. It's Malvolia Du Mal," Jamie thought. He was about to call Mack when the back door crashed wide open, almost thrown off its hinges. At the same moment Mack appeared at the door to the middle room. Of course, Jamie thought, Mack had felt Malvolia's presence even while Jamie was making the tea. There was something rather terrible about Mack as he stood facing the back door, his white cane raised like a sword. Something comical too, since Fern was there, peeping round his legs.

Karrax was so excited by the sight of the malevolent Malvolia filling the doorway that he had started a small blizzard. Flakes were swirling around the little room and the temperature was steadily dropping.

Malvolia placed her hands on her hips. "Step aside, old man," she snarled at Mack through the whirling snow. "I want the dragon."

Karrax's growling had risen to a squawk, and there was a bright spot of white fire burning in his eyes.

"Go away you fat horrible smelly woman!" Fern yelled from the safety of Mack's legs.

Malvolia raised an eyebrow and addressed the Chilldrake, whose grip was bringing tears to Jamie's eyes.

"And don't think of disappearing," she hissed. "If you do I'll not guarantee the safety of your new little friends."

Mack extended his cane and touched Malvolia on the shoulder. "Get thee gone, Sorceress," he said. "Thou shalt not pass me."

"Yes," Fern shouted, innocent of the danger. "Push thee off, you pink hippo!"

Jamie couldn't move. Malvolia stepped into the kitchen. Apart from the terrible flash of anger in her eyes, she seemed quite ordinary. And yet, perhaps it was her terrible, sickly-sweet scent (which was overpowering and rotten when she came close) that suggested her suppressed evil.

"Do something, Mack!" Jamie shouted. "We can't give her Karrax. You said you were a wizard. Can't you get rid of her?"

Malvolia gave a shriek of laughter that set Jamie's teeth on edge.

"Wizard?" she echoed. "Is that what McGee told you? Well, maybe he was, once. Don't you know, little boy, that a wizard's magic – such as it is – is all in his eyes? This blind old fool has about as much power as a flat battery. But then, I don't suppose for one moment that he told you that. Just as I don't suppose he told you that we once practised magic together!"

Jamie looked at Mack, waiting for him to say it wasn't so. Mack stood still with his cane held before him, saying nothing. Malvolia smiled. "Oh yes, we are old friends, are we not, McGee?" and then she contradicted herself. "No, not friends, never friends. Partners, would you say, McGee? And we would be still, only you had to overreach yourself. You had to try and strike out on your own. And look where that got you, you old fool. Blind and powerless. I shall not make the same mistakes that you did, McGee. Now, get out of my way! I've come for the dragon."

She knocked Mack to one side and sent him sprawling over the top of Fern, who had suddenly become more of a hindrance than a help.

Jamie backed away as Malvolia entered the kitchen, until his back was against the cooker. Malvolia took a deep breath and stepped over Mack and Fern who were slithering about on the floor.

"She's going to stretch!" Fern yelled, scrabbling about in the drifting snow. "Run, Jamie, run!"

And Jamie did. Or rather, he tried to, but for the second time that morning his feet slid in the snow and, still with Karrax clinging to his shoulder, he fell to his knees.

As Jamie tried to steady himself and rise, Malvolia reached out, grasping the Chilldrake's wing with one hand and Jamie about the throat with her other. Karrax struggled and drew blood as his talons sank into Jamie's shoulder. Jamie felt Malvolia's fingers squeeze like a vice against his windpipe, and the room started to spin. Fern, untangling herself from Mack's legs, scrambled forward and tugged at Malvolia's hand, trying to prise the witch's fingers from Jamie's throat.

"Mack!" she squealed. "Do something! She's choking Jim."

Mack tried to get up, and half-succeeded, when Malvolia turned her head, her eyes filled with a dreadful light. She opened her mouth and uttered a sound from the back of her throat. A blast of foul wind struck Mack and smashed him against the wall. Fern didn't know what to do. She could see Jamie's eyes start to close, his face almost purple. Fern clamped her teeth on to Malvolia's hand, biting as hard as he could. Mack, rousing himself, groped for Fern to drag her away. Malvolia tried frantically to shake Fern loose from her hand, and at the same time wrench Karrax from Jamie's shoulder. Fern's jaws clenched with a desperate strength, but Malvolia's grip was stronger. A few seconds more and Jamie would be unconscious, or worse.

And then Mack cried out desperately, "*Geharran Mittakar Karrax! Druin na berred Essillar!*"

The little Chilldrake froze at the strange words, its eyes narrowing to slits. It raised its head and screeched at Malvolia, who was grunting with both the pain of Fern's bite and the effort of trying to part Karrax and Jamie.

"*Geharran Mittakar! Khorovindt!*" Mack called again, and there was a fierce note of command in his voice.

Suddenly the terrible panic of not being able to breathe ended and Jamie gasped with relief as the pain eased in his bursting chest. There was a sudden boom, like thunder, and instantly the kitchen was emptied of snow and Malvolia Du Mal, leaving Mack, Fern and Jamie bewildered and alone.

Karrax had obeyed Mack's awful command, uttered in Mithacan. The Chilldrake had skipped and, in doing so, he had taken Malvolia to Mithaca.

8

Mum Wakes

"They're terrible bruises," said Fern, as she stared at Jamie's neck. "Mum'll think I tried to do you in."

She was sitting nursing her tooth, running her tongue along the bit that was chipped and wincing every time she found the raw nerve. She could still taste Malvolia's soapy scent on her lips and not even the chocolate biscuits that she nibbled on the good side of her mouth could get rid of it.

"Will Karrax be all right, Mr Mack? She won't kill him, will she?" Fern asked.

Mack put down his mug. "Goodness no, Fern," he said, but there was no mistaking the tone of forced bravery in Mack's voice. "Karrax is too useful to Malvolia. She's not so rash that she would harm the only thing that could carry her between worlds."

"But she doesn't need to return here," said Jamie. "She's there, in Mithaca, where she always wanted to be, to rule and to have power. Why should she want to get back?"

"It was all so sudden," said Mack, and his voice sounded faraway and lost. Then he shook himself. Jamie couldn't decide whether he was explaining or apologising for what had happened. "Malvolia wasn't expecting to be taken into Mithaca so suddenly. She's not in the least prepared for it. She doesn't know the place. It will be as much a shock for her to know she has gone as it was for us to see her go."

"Karrax did it to save us, didn't he, Mr Mack?" Fern asked. "It's just the thing that Buzz Beddows would have done. You know, gone into danger to save the rest of the Stargang. That's what you shouted to him in French, wasn't it? Something like 'Take the stinking witch away'?"

Mack smiled despite his own miserable thoughts. "Something like that. And it wasn't French," Mack said and he stood up. "I think it's time I woke your mother."

"Just like that?" Jamie said, feeling a sudden surge of uncontrollable emotion. "I mean, that's it? You're just going to wake Mum, and then leave?" He could feel his cheeks getting red with anger. "Just wake Mum up and go home, when Karrax's life may be in danger, because it might, whatever you say. Just wake Mum and leave everything as it was before? Malvolia recognised you on the corner. She came back because she knew you were here, and now you're running away. Do you want her to think that she's beaten you? Don't you want to help Karrax?"

Mack bowed his head at Jamie's sudden outburst.

"I didn't say I was leaving," he said. "The only way that we could possibly help both Karrax and Mithaca would be to finish Malvolia once and for all. And, unless she happens to use Karrax to come back, then the only way we could even hope to stop her would be to go to Mithaca. Karrax isn't the only one who can take us there. That's why I want to wake your mother. She— "

"You're a fraud," said Jamie, before Mack could say any more. "A fraud and a coward!"

Fern's mouth dropped open at Jamie's rudeness. Mack raised himself to his full height. "If you were ten years older, young man, I should knock you to the floor for saying that."

"It's true," Jamie said. "Anyway, we don't want any more help from you. You can just leave Mum alone and get out."

"But you said we would still be friends," Fern cried. "You said we would. You don't have to listen to Jamie; he isn't always right, and he isn't right now. He's just being hateful because he's angry. You can still be *my* friend."

"If you won't take me to your mother," Mack said to Jamie, "will you at least get me my cane?"

"It's broken," Jamie said. "It broke when you fell over trying to run away."

"Stop it, Jim!" Fern cried. "Mack wasn't trying to run. He was doing his best to save you. *You're* the liar, not Mack. You— '

Fern stopped suddenly, her eyes fixed on the doorway to the parlour. Mrs Mercer stood there, her hands pressed to the sides of her head. Jamie cast a quick, unfriendly glance at Mack and then went to help his mother. Together they came into the middle room. Mrs Mercer was squinting as if even the dull light was hurting her eyes. She blinked several times and then stared hard at Mack as if waiting for an explanation for this stranger in her home.

"This is Mr McGee," said Jamie reluctantly. "He was just leaving."

"Mack's our friend," said Fern loyally, moving to stand by the old man. Mrs Mercer sank slowly on to a chair and looked up at Mack's face. She frowned, raising a hand to her lips.

"McGee?" she whispered. "Caspar McGee?"

Mack held out a hand. "Oh no," said Mrs Mercer. "No polite handshakes, McGee. I know what you're here for." Her voice rose to a shout. "And I'll be damned if I'll let you have it after all these years!"

Fern looked at Jamie, whose expression had changed from one of sullen indifference to one of utter amazement. He shook his head. Like Fern, he hadn't the faintest idea what was going on.

Mack took a deep breath. Even he seemed unable to understand why Mrs Mercer should know him. Her anger at his being there was just as incomprehensible. Mrs Mercer was staring at him with cold eyes. Jamie asked the question.

"How do you know him, Mum?" he said.

"I know *of* him," Mrs Mercer replied. "I just wish I didn't. And I don't know how he wheedled his way in here, but the sooner he leaves the better."

Fern's loyalty remained unshaken. "Mack's done nothing wrong," she protested. "I don't know why everyone's being rotten to him. He even sent the witch away, at least he told Karrax to."

At the mention of the Chilldrake's name, Mrs Mercer jumped. "You mean he was here? Karrax was here? When? Tell me when. Is he here now? Why didn't you tell me before? And what witch?"

Fern swallowed hard and gave a fast and slightly garbled version of the visit and the transformation of Miss Dummel and how Mack had wiped it from her mind.

"I see," Mrs Mercer said to Mack. "And doubtless you tried to make me forget a lot more besides. Luckily, some memories go back a lot further than you can reach, Caspar McGee. Did you tell me about the Chilldrake this morning, Fern? Has he made me 'forget' that too?"

"Jamie told *me* not to," said Fern.

"I tried to," said Jamie. "I said there was a lizard and I said there was snow, only you weren't listening. You never do listen. I don't know what's going on. I wish somebody would explain."

"Enough," said Mack, and his voice was stern. "Enough. Your opinion of me at the moment, Mrs Mercer, must be based on what you may have heard of me in the past. I can assure you that it no longer applies. I have not come here *for* anything. I met your son in the library. He was trying to find out about Chilldrakes. I merely offered to help."

"I've heard about your sort of help. More like helping yourself," said Mrs Mercer. Fern and Jamie sat down. It had been ages since their mother had shown anything like this spirit. Fern thought she sounded just like Jade-Sola from the Stargang, all fizzing and ready for a fight with anyone.

"It is clear that you have met with Karrax yourself, in the past," Mack said, feeling for a chair. "Do you mind if I sit? I must confess the thought that he might once have appeared to you did not occur to me." Mack wiped a hand across his forehead. "So much has happened so quickly, and after such a long time. I don't know what you have heard about me" – he held up a hand for silence when he heard Mrs Mercer take a breath to speak – "but, please, please believe that I mean no one any harm. Not any more. I am too old, I am too tired and, if it's not too strange a thing to say, my eyes were opened the day that they were taken away."

Mrs Mercer pursed her lips warily, though the cold distrust had gone from her eyes. "Explain exactly who you are to the children, then," she said. "Maybe I'll listen and understand the change of heart you say you've had. Then again, maybe I won't. But I'll give you the chance, Caspar McGee."

"Thank you for that, at least," he said. Then he turned to where Jamie and Fern were sitting. He was silent for some moments, gathering his thoughts, and then he began.

"A long time ago, long before even I or your mother come into this story, the boundaries of this world and the boundaries of Mithaca were not so – not so separate or so far apart. In fact it would be not uncommon for people and things to pass from one world to the other. Oh, not quite as quickly as Karrax is able to do – in that respect Karrax is a one-off. But there were ways, secret groves, certain hills, small places hidden away and guarded, that were sort of doorways between Mithaca and here, and men accepted them quite naturally, *and* they were not afraid of the things that they saw there."

"What sort of things?" Fern asked.

"You have heard of unicorns, hippogriffs, trolls – dragons?" Mack said. Fern and Jamie nodded together. "All those sorts of things, and more; things that we now keep pressed between the pages of a legend, like dried flowers that still have a little of their colour and an echo of the life that they once had. Anyway, for a time, for a long time, these two worlds touched and then . . ."

"And then?" Jamie prompted.

"And then men found things that they thought were better," said Mack quickly.

Jamie heard his mother give a snort of derision. But she let Mack continue.

"Things like, oh . . ."

"Dishwashers!" suggested Fern.

"Yes, in a way," Mack said. "At least, Science. Well, not even that really. The point I'm trying to make is that men forgot that things like magic and unicorns and dragons ever truly existed. They gave them over to children and fairy-tales, and all the old doorways closed for ever."

"Some remember," said Mrs Mercer grimly. "Evil beings like Malvolia Du Mal would like to get to Mithaca and get their hands on what's there to twist it to their own miserable and greedy ends. And now she *is* there, doing Lord knows what damage, and it's more than partly due to Caspar McGee. It isn't the first time that someone has tried to take over Mithaca, though somebody ought to make sure that it's the last time."

"Mum?" Jamie said quietly, unable to disguise the wonder in his voice. "How do you know about all these things?"

"Karrax told me about the first attempt to take over Mithaca," Mrs Mercer said simply. "When I was seven or eight. He told me when he brought me the— ' She paused and looked suddenly at Mack, blushing as if she had just blundered into giving away a secret. "I don't mean 'told' in the sense you think," she said, changing the subject quickly. "I sort of understood what he said all those years ago." She stopped and addressed Mack. "Do you want to carry on, or shall I?"

"It's quite all right, Mrs Mercer. You tell the children. I don't mind . . . " Mack said.

"There was once a magician," said Mrs Mercer. "He thought himself a great magician and, by chance, he came across Karrax while he was on one of his 'skips' out of Mithaca. He persuaded Karrax to take him into his world. And when he got there and learned about the power that was available for the taking he – well,

I suppose you could say that it all went to his head; he got carried away, like you do when you see something that you want too much. Of course there were those who resented the magician's attempt to barge in and take over, and it started a terrible war."

"Can't have been all that much of a war," Fern said. "The whole of Mithaca against one magician."

"All wars are terrible," said Mrs Mercer. "The magician had great magic of his own. A dark magic that drew all the dark things of Mithaca to him. Every world has both its good and bad and there were those that gathered round him, to help him and to enrich themselves with the pickings at the end. Things that weren't really bad but just weak in themselves followed him. Creatures like the Scad— "

"They call themselves the Scedharmaun," Mack interrupted in a soft voice. "But Skoddermen will do. In Mithacan it means 'weak of will' and while generally they keep to themselves and do little harm, they can be . . . persuaded . . . by one means or another to perform certain tasks that they wouldn't normally undertake."

"Thank you. As you say, Skoddermen," said Mrs Mercer.

Mack sat quietly back in the armchair, his chin resting on one hand. Mrs Mercer cast him a brief glance and then continued. "At the very centre of Mithaca was its Heart, a thing of great power in that world, and the magician learned that once he got his hands on that then there would be nothing anyone could do to stop him proclaiming himself the sole and unchallengeable Lord of Mithaca. The Chilldrakes knew it too, so the one with the ability to do so, that's Karrax, removed the Heart of Mithaca from its resting place, and he brought it into this world, unknown and unseen by anyone, except me that is."

"And left it with you!" Jamie cried, glimpsing now a reason for the Chilldrake's appearance. "He gave you the Heart of Mithaca? Why, why did he decide to leave it with you? And why did he wait so long to come back for it?"

"Can I see it?" said Fern. "And what happened to the magician? Did he ever find the Heart was gone?"

"He found that it had gone," said Mack. "But he didn't know where, not until now."

"I remember the day that he came," Mrs Mercer said. "I was sitting underneath an old tree in your grandmother's garden. It was late summer. I don't recall what I was doing or why I was there but suddenly there was snow, thick and fast, falling from the branches. I looked up and there he was, the Heart in his beak, filling my mind with so many thoughts and ideas that I thought I was going mad. I was no older than Fern is now and, for that reason perhaps, I readily accepted all the oddity and the strangeness and the wonder of it. We talked of many, many things, and Karrax left the Heart of Mithaca with me because – because . . . " she paused and seemed unable to continue.

"Karrax left the Heart with your mother," said Mack, "because of her Mithacan blood."

Fern's jaw dropped open and Jamie's eyes grew wide with disbelief. Mrs Mercer nodded.

"McGee has already told you that long ago men crossed the borders of this world and Mithaca. Well, it worked both ways. Some Mithacans came to this world. Some remained long after the old doors were closed."

"Then, then . . . " Jamie said, " . . . that makes me and Fern Mithacan too. A little bit of us anyway."

"Wait till I tell Sarah Mellor," Fern said. "She'll go green and die. But you didn't say what happened to the magician, Mack."

"They put out his eyes," said Mack in a hollow voice. "They put out his eyes so that his darker powers were gone. And Karrax brought him back to this world. Oh, he was forgiven. They bear no grudges in Mithaca, and robbing him of most of his powers was the worst punishment of all. He went to one of his old pupils, Malvolia, and she looked after him for a while, until she learned of Mithaca, until she started to burn with her own desire to get there and triumph where her former master had failed, and she set off on her own dark quest to look for the skipper, Karrax. The little Chilldrake couldn't help himself, you see. He would keep skipping between worlds. Alone, the blind magician started to rebuild what was left of his life. He had learned, while in Mithaca, of the possibility that some people in this world might have Mithacan ancestors. He wanted to find those descendants and tell them, warn them that Malvolia was seeking to take over the land of their father's fathers. He didn't know that there was anything they could do about it, but he felt that he had to try. He felt that it would make amends, somehow."

Mack paused briefly and smiled to himself.

"I was getting close too, Mrs Mercer. It wasn't easy, being blind, to trace back through old and forgotten records. I had to beg librarians and churchwardens not only to dig out ancient papers, but to read them to me as well. It was pure chance that Jamie and I met in the library. But I like to think that, sooner or later, we would have met anyway."

"Oh, Mack," said Fern. "You were once a baddie, like Revoltron."

"And who's to say he's changed?" said Jamie.

Mack suddenly started to laugh. "To think that the Heart was here," he said. "Under Malvolia's nose all the time. With that in her possession she wouldn't have had need of Karrax at all. It is said that the Heart can bridge both worlds. I only wish I could see her face when she finds out we have it."

"But she won't find out we have it," said Jamie. "She's in Mithaca and the Heart is here. Can't we leave it like that? Won't Mithaca be safe while the Heart is here and she's there? Karrax wouldn't tell her anything, I know he wouldn't. No matter what she did to him."

"Mithaca safe?" said Mack. "Not with Malvolia there, Jamie. She has the power to wreak enough havoc on her own, without the Heart. And don't underestimate Malvolia's intelligence either. When she finds out that the Heart isn't in its rightful place then she's sure to guess where it might be. Don't forget that she's seen both the Chilldrake and me here. Two add two adds up to six: number six Stubbs Terrace."

"You're right," said Mrs Mercer, "much as I hate to admit it. Sooner or later she'll reason what's happened. Whatever destruction she can do on her own, she wants, more than anything, the limitless power of the Heart. What we ought to do, if we care enough, is to get to Mithaca and surrender the Heart to those who know how to use it to save their own world. At the very least, I think we owe it to Karrax to repay his trust and his bravery. You told me how he saved Jamie's life, Fern. By doing so, he put his own world at risk whether he knew it or not. And don't forget there's Mithacan blood in our veins. It may not be pure, but it's there all the same. The least we can do is to try and return the Heart to people who'll know best how to use it to save Mithaca from Malvolia."

"Go to Mithaca?" Jamie said. "We can't, not unless Karrax takes us. Or can we?"

"The Heart itself will take you there," said Mack. "I can show you how . . . if you'll let me help." He looked to Mrs Mercer but she was gazing at the children, as if she was seeing them for the first time and with new eyes. She saw Jamie, his face alight with wonder at the thought of travelling to the world from where the ancestors had come in the dim and distant past. She saw Fern, small and wiry, whose eyes were filled with concern for the blind old magician.

She stood suddenly. She looked tall, strong and graceful. "You say you wanted to help, McGee," she said. "You say you've changed. May the Mithacans forgive me if I'm wrong, but I'm willing to trust you. You've been to Mithaca before. You know the place and if, *if* we manage to get ourselves there then we'll need your knowledge. What do you say? Will you come with us?"

Fern knew what Mack's answer would be and she couldn't understand why everyone stayed so serious when Mack slowly nodded his head.

9

Into Mithaca

Of course the first thing that they needed was the Heart itself. Mrs Mercer disappeared upstairs to fetch it. While she was gone Jamie and Fern talked in low whispers.

"This is better than a dream," said Fern. "You can only wake up from dreams, no matter how good they are."

"Let's hope," Jamie said, "that it doesn't turn into a nightmare."

Fern followed Jamie's gaze to where Mack was sitting at the other side of the room, his long fingers pressed together and his face turned away, as if he was in deep thought or prayer.

"You don't trust him at all, do you?" Fern whispered.

"I don't know," said Jamie. "I suppose people can change."

"Mum's changed," said Fern. "You can see it in her eyes. Can you imagine her being a little girl and seeing Karrax too, all those years ago? I wonder if she ever told Gran. And why did she never talk about it to us?"

"I don't know," Jamie confessed. "I only know how hard I found it when I tried to tell Mum this morning. Perhaps Mum did try to tell Gran, though if she listened

I don't suppose she would have believed Mum. And as for not telling us . . . " he added, "well, kids grow up. They forget things. You can't even remember what you did last week."

"She kept the Heart though!" Fern said. "Isn't it exciting? Do you think we'll go now, right this minute?"

Mrs Mercer answered Fern's question by returning at that moment with a large hold-all over one shoulder and a small box clutched in her right hand.

"The puzzle box!" Jamie said, seeing the small wooden cube that his mother was holding. It had always been on his mother's dressing table ever since he could remember. It was made of various types of wood, slotted together in such a way that only by sliding certain pieces in and out at different stages would the lid eventually lift off to reveal the contents. Jamie had often played with it when he was younger and he had heard the rattle of contents whenever the box was shaken, but he had never succeeded in finding the right sequence of moves that would open it.

"A birthday present from my mother," said Mrs Mercer. "I just hope that I can remember how to open it when the time comes. What do we do, Mack?" said Mrs Mercer. She saw Jamie's eyebrows raise on hearing her being friendly to the old man. "We have the Heart; how do we use it to get to Mithaca?"

Mack turned his black-shielded eyes to Jamie and Fern's mum.

"Will yourself there," said Mack. "With all the concentration you can manage. Try and imagine the Heart returning home and you, us, going with it."

"That's not much," said Jamie, unimpressed. "Aren't there any spells or chants?"

"Not for this part," said Mack darkly. "Mrs Mercer?"

"Louise," said Mrs Mercer. "I'd feel better if you called me Louise."

Mack nodded. "Louise, will you take out the Heart?"

Mrs Mercer frowned and bit her lip. She turned the box in her hands, trying first to remember which was the correct way to hold it. Finally satisfied, she slid out one small panel, pushed in a second, and turned the top half of the box clockwise in her fingers. She twisted one bottom corner, depressed a third inlaid square and was rewarded with a tiny "click". She lifted the freed lid of the little box and tipped out the contents into her palm.

Fern thought that Mrs Mercer would take out of the small box a real, live, beating (and probably bleeding) heart. Jamie wasn't quite sure what to expect. He thought that the Heart of Mithaca might be a large ruby or something equally as precious. And neither could hide their sense of disappointment when their mother took out and held up a small, round pebble, brown and dull and lifeless. It looked the sort of thing that anyone might have picked up from any beach, any street, any building site, and tossed away as nothing. Mrs Mercer noticed their frowns and understood.

"Doesn't look much, does it?" she said. "I can remember showing it to Grandad and telling him what I had been told it was. He said that I had a vivid imagination." Her voice fell to a whisper. "The Heart of Mithaca."

Jamie poked it with a finger. It was cold and uninteresting.

"What do you think, Mum?" he asked. "Do you reckon this pebble can take us to another world, just by thinking about it? You really believe that's the Heart of Mithaca?"

"Well," said Mrs Mercer slowly, "Karrax brought it

to me and he told me as much and you have to believe that, or we might as well give up now. Without Karrax, this is the only way we can enter Mithaca."

"Gather round your mother, children," Mack said. He took a hand in each of his and Jamie and Fern locked theirs in a circle about their mother. Mrs Mercer smiled encouragingly at Jamie and said, "Ready?"

Fern nodded her head quickly, running the tip of her tongue over her tooth where it was chipped. If fat pink women could disappear when you had your teeth in their hands, then she was quite ready to call a pebble a Heart. Jamie closed his eyes and thought of Karrax. If Karrax had brought that pebble and told his mum that it was the Heart of Mithaca then it must be true because Karrax was true. He closed his eyes and waited.

They all waited a long time. Jamie thought for one, brief second how daft they must look, and then he pushed the thought angrily from his mind, afraid that it would spoil whatever magic might be trying to work. As his flicker of doubt died he felt a warm wind on his face and knew that they were on their way. And yet he refused to look in case the only sight that met his eyes was the dreary parlour of the house in Stubbs Terrace.

Fern kept her eyes open and she tried afterwards to describe what she saw. It was as if the parlour wasn't at all real but a rather dull picture painted on a canvas with paint that was still wet. As she watched, all the colours, or rather all the greys and the browns and the drab yellows of the walls, started to run from the top of the room to the bottom. And as they sluiced away and dripped and melted into the floor Fern saw the twinkling of stars in a midnight sky beyond. There wasn't the swoosh of Karrax's skip, only the soft sigh of a wind through trees far away on the horizon, and the distant gurgle of a stream somewhere close by.

For Mrs Mercer it was different again. She had her eyes fixed upon the Heart, and it was as if the small pebble slowly grew large as a screen on which she saw, like a film running backwards, her whole life, all of it, beginning with her opening the puzzle box. As she stared the images quickened and the film ran faster and faster through that day and then yesterday, faster and faster until all her yesterdays were a brilliant blur on the stone's smooth surface. Back through time the film ran, stopping abruptly at length, at the frame which showed a small girl, not unlike Fern, staring into the blue-faceted eyes of a little Chilldrake.

Mack; Mack saw nothing of course, but he too felt a clean and warm wind ripple through his hair. There was a tingling in the scars of his sightless eyes that grew steadily into a fierce pain that he had only felt once before and which he never thought he would feel again. The pain increased into a terrible stabbing and right at the point where he felt he could bear it no longer, at the point when he thought he must surely let go of Jamie's hand and scream in agony, the pain stopped.

Jamie opened his eyes and saw moonlight. He blinked, like someone waking from a deep sleep, desperate to remember his first impression of this other world, where long ago ancestors of his had walked.

Silver moonbeams split the dark, scudding clouds overhead, and washed everything with its pale reflected shine. He saw only the white and the grey and the black; the white of the moonshine, the grey of the lighter shadows, and the black of the deeper spaces where the moonlight could not reach. Somewhere, in another place, the little parlour of Stubbs Terrace stood empty and cold. Here and now, the fresh wind of Mithaca blew and ruffled his hair.

"It's just like the park," said Fern, breaking the circle of hands.

"Not like the park," said Mrs Mercer, slipping the heart back into the puzzle box and closing it. She slipped the box into a deep pocket of the hold-all. "Not at all like the park. We must be very careful. This is wild and open country."

"Watch out for cow-muck," Fern giggled, and then she saw her mother's stern and slightly worried face in the moonlight.

"Wild and open country," Mrs Mercer repeated slowly. "And full of places and creatures that may be dangerous."

Dangerous? What did his mum mean by dangerous? thought Jamie. This was Mithaca, this was Karrax's home. And then he caught sight of Mack and remembered that the folk of this place had once put out his eyes. No doubt at the time they did it for the best reason of all . . . *and*, he thought suddenly, what if they met someone or something that remembered Mack from the last time? Wouldn't they automatically think that he, that they all, were there for the wrong reason? He, Fern and his mother were strangers here after all. Yes, on reflection, it probably was dangerous.

Fern shuddered with glee. "Why is it night?" she asked. "It was only the afternoon a minute ago."

"We entered by means of the Heart," Mack said. "There's always a price to pay when you tap its power. We have lost some time."

"What now, now we're here?" Jamie asked. Mrs

Mercer stared through the moonlit shadows. Mack was breathing deeply in the still air.

"We proceed with care and caution," he said. "And I think the first thing we must do is to find help."

"What sort of help?" Fern asked. "Can't we just follow Malvolia and get Karrax back? I thought that's what we came here for."

"We came to find someone who could use the Heart to destroy Malvolia, clod," said Jamie. "Do you never listen?"

"We *did* come to save Karrax, pig," Fern replied.

"So we did," said Mack. "And so we will, in time. But the four of us couldn't hope to confront Malvolia alone. And I wouldn't want to run into her right at this moment, not with what your mother has in her bag."

"But nor can we afford to lose all trace of her," said Mrs Mercer. "Standing about and calling each other names isn't a sensible way to begin. I vote that we try and follow her at a safe distance. That way, at least, we have some hope of keeping track of what her plans might be, rather than if we ran round looking for some vague sort of assistance."

Even Mack couldn't think of a better suggestion, but which way was the best way? Mrs Mercer stared about her in the moonlight.

"Where in Mithaca are we anyway, Mack?" she asked. Mack knelt and pulled grass from the ground. He pressed it to his face and inhaled the scent and rubbed it against his face.

"Mairm-grass," he said. "Tough and coarse. It grows profusely on the Midplain. I'd say we want to head south and east."

"Why?" Jamie asked.

"It is the direction Malvolia should be heading," Mack replied.

"I don't know if it's south-east or not," Mrs Mercer said suddenly, "but that's the way they went."

Jamie followed his mother's pointing finger. On the ground and shining in the moonlight like the track of a snail was a trail of silver crystals.

"What is it? What can you see?" Mack asked.

"It's frost," Jamie said. "Karrax's frost. It starts where the kitchen would be in our own world, and it carries right on over the hills as far as I can see. He's left us a trail to follow."

"I think we should have sat in a taxi when we came to Mithaca," said Fern as they started to trudge off into the night. "And then the taxi would have come too and we shouldn't have had to walk."

"Oh, brilliant," said Jamie, guiding Mack as best he could over the uneven ground. "And quite apart from scaring the driver out of his skin, the whole of Mithaca, good or bad, would hear the engine and come running."

Fern sighed and resigned herself to saving her breath for the hill climb. She held Mack's hand, half leading and half dragging him through the night, while Jamie and Mrs Mercer took the lead, their eyes and ears straining for the slightest movement or the faintest noise in the darkness.

For almost two hours they walked in silence and silver darkness, following the frosty track that Karrax had left. The Midplain was all open ground, with only a few dark clumps of trees to break the monotony. In the bright moonlight, the track was easy to follow, though in places the trail thinned out and threatened to fail, as if the little Chilldrake was so tired that he could make no more frost, and then, after some searching and a good deal of luck, they would pick up the track of frost again in the moonlight; each time there was less and less of it.

"There's something wrong with Karrax," thought Jamie, and then he realised with relief that the frost was simply melting with the approach of morning. Away to the east there was a dull grey light that slowly deepened to the bright yellow of dawn, as the brilliant sun of Sunday morning rose over the far hills of Mithaca. A little after sunrise the trail of frost melted away completely. There was no more to follow.

The four of them stood on the brow of a hill and looked over a low plain stretching away to the purple-topped mountains that ringed the horizon like broken teeth. There was no sign of any movement in the still morning, save for a few early birds that swooped in the upper airs, circling in ever-descending spirals as if they were coming down for a look.

"No sign of anything or anyone," said Mrs Mercer. "Only crows. Malvolia had a good start on us." She rummaged in the depths of the handbag, drawing out a flask and a package wrapped in the paper from a loaf.

"Breakfast, I think," she said, and then a sudden thought struck her as she caught sight again of the crows wheeling in flight. "Are crows good or bad here, Mack?" she asked in a low voice that the children couldn't hear.

"Indifferent, for the most part," Mack replied. "I never found any real use for them anyway." Mrs Mercer silently thanked him for his honesty.

They were all hungry, and they shared out the sandwiches that Mrs Mercer had hurriedly prepared. Mack and Mrs Mercer drank coffee as the sun climbed higher and the sky turned from grey to blue.

It was odd, thought Jamie. Odd and beautiful and

strange. As far as he could see there was countryside. Green and rolling hills and small woods and thin streamlets all tumbling through the landscape. No walls, no fences, no houses, no roads and no traffic.

"Because there's no Science," he said, and then flushed to think he had spoken his thought aloud.

"Science is no bad thing, you know, Jim," said Mack, picking up on Jamie's thoughts. "In our own world we've benefited a lot from it. It's like magic though, like any power, too much of it and too much misuse of it, and things start to drift. Men's heads get turned, and their hearts get a little colder to the wonder of it. I should know . . . "

"I wasn't thinking of anything that you might have done," Jamie said coldly. "Though it's hard to see why anybody could look at anything as unspoiled as this and then want to claim it for their own."

Mack sighed and sipped at his coffee. A sudden gust of fresh wind lifted the now empty loaf-wrapper and blew it down into a thicket of small trees and shrubs. Jamie jumped up, grateful for the interruption.

"I'll get it," he called and, before anyone could argue, he raced down after the litter. He ran a short way into the thicket and stopped, hearing his mother call out for him to be careful.

The close hush of the copse enfolded him like a blanket. There was no breeze there and small motes of dust rose and fell and spun in the shafts of light that broke through the greenery overhead. Jamie cast about him for the bread-wrapper. There it was; a bright splash of pillarbox-red, caught in the branches of a straggling thorn. Jamie stepped over, grabbed at the wrapper and snatched it out.

"You . . . you . . . you gangling gawk!" a gruff voice

bellowed. "You clod-whomping swidge of gornling snottage. You trodging glob of swimping shlock! Give me back my hat before I strump you so hard you'll end up in next Wednesday, flat on your fimpling swimmocks!"

Jamie was so startled that he jumped back a step and stared at what he thought was the bread-wrapper in his hand. It was red, but it was no bread-wrapper. It was a small hat and it was its owner who was making all the noise.

"I'm sorry!" Jamie gasped, and he dropped the hat as if it was electrified.

"Oh, thank *you*," said the voice from the bush. "That's right, flirk it in the mudge. I mean, it isn't as if it was clean on this morning or anything!"

The bush rustled and the branches parted and a man no taller than Jamie's knees stepped out. He wore clothes of such an indistinct green that he blended in with his surroundings, so that only his face and hands (and his red hat) were properly visible. His face was old and brown as leather, but he looked at Jamie with large green eyes that were ageless and clear. He picked up the hat, brushed it clean of dirt and twigs and jammed it on his head.

"You think you own this place, you Murglings," he said, only a fraction calmer for having retrieved his property. "You whomp about, churning up wilth with your great domping feet, pinching a body's headgear, without the slightest . . . " The little man stopped. "Did you pollerjise just then?"

Jamie nodded dumbly. The little man crossed his arms and sniffed. "Can't be a Murgling then. They never so much as pass the time of day, or so my old dadder used to say. They just eats yer then spits out the gritty-bones. What are you, a hodge-goblin?"

"Do I look like one?" said Jamie, a little less afraid of the owner of the loud voice and peculiar speech.

"Can't say. Never seen one," the man replied. "Never seen a Murgling neither come to think of it. In fact, first time I've had my hat sprotted. Heh! Bit of an adventure, what!"

He stepped forward and a big smile creased his already wrinkled face.

"Name's Pinch. Sorry I whoomed at yer. You caught me by surprise. Fact is, I was dozing and I should have been on guard for Skoddermen, but that's just atwix you an' me." He flicked out a hand and caught Jamie's forefinger, shaking it almost enough to work it loose.

"No hard feelings, eh, skimpling?"

"None at all," said Jamie. In fact, he rather thought that he had just found their first friend in Mithaca.

10

Pinch

"I'm Jamie Mercer," Jamie said, pulling back his finger from Pinch's grasp. It felt numb from all the shaking.

"Pleased to meet yer," said Pinch, and then he stood with his hands behind his back, staring at Jamie with his large green eyes as if he was waiting for him to do something.

"You're not from these parts are you, skimpling?" said Pinch, frowning a little. Jamie shook his head.

"Not really," he admitted. "That is, it seems that my I-don't-know-how-many-times-great-grandfather was, but we only came here a short while ago, from . . . " What should he say? From Earth? From the real world? "From Stubbs Terrace," he said.

Pinch scratched his head. "Stubsterris?" he said. "New to me, skimpling. Still, if they all pollerjise as lordish as you in Stubsterris, then it can't be a bad place. What you mean, we?"

"We?" Jamie repeated, and then, "Oh, we! Yes, I came with Mum and Fern and Mack. We . . . " Jamie thought frantically for the right expression. "We are on a quest, sort of."

Pinch nodded approvingly. "Quests is good. Quests is what every young skimpling and their Mumanfern-anmack should go on." He set his wrinkled head on one side and said, “What’s a quest, skimpling?”

Jamie smiled and was about to try and explain when his mum and Fern and Mack strode into the thicket. Pinch jumped and resumed his aggressive manner. He raised his little fists and stood between Jamie and the three newcomers, as if he was going to take them all on in one fight.

“Come on then, murglings,” he cried, waving his fists like a miniature boxer. “Come on! I’ll smadge you to dobs. Stay behind me, Jamie Mercer. These murglings look mean and gangly.”

“No wait,” said Jamie, who couldn’t help but smile. “These are the friends I told you about. This is Mum and my sister Fern, and Mack.”

Pinch lowered his fists. “Look like murglings to me,” he said eyeing them warily. “Especially the gloomling one with the white spilth. What’s wrong with his eyes? Why have they got lids on?” Mack frowned as if he was trying to place the sound of Pinch’s voice and Mrs Mercer seemed uncomfortable. Fern ran forward and knelt down in front of Pinch so that her face was on a level with his.

“He’s lovely,” she said. “Can I pick him up? What’s his name?”

Pinch crossed his arms and scowled, dodging out of the way of Fern’s grasping hands. “Why?” he asked Jamie. “Why does the small ugly one talk about me as if I am not here? Is she simple? Are her brains whiffled?”

Fern squealed with delight, not in the least bit annoyed at being called simple. Then Mrs Mercer stepped forward.

“I am Louise Mercer, and these are my children, Jamie and Fern. The tall – erm – gloomling one is

Mack. We are strangers here, but we would like to be friends. And we badly need help and guidance."

She held out her hand and Pinch shook it warmly. "Glad to know where we stand, Looey Smurser. I am Pinch. Keeper of the Copse and Boscage Abouts. And what can I do for my new palsomes and friendlies?"

Pinch studied their strange clothes, sprang on to a small branch of a bush and sat swinging his legs, waiting for an answer.

"We're looking for a fat, pink . . . ow!" Fern winced as Jamie kicked her shin.

"We are looking for a woman called Malvolia," said Mrs Mercer. "She has kidnapped another friend of ours, and we are afraid that she may do him harm."

"I see," Pinch said, taking off his hat and fanning himself as he swung. He seemed preoccupied with Mack and his dark glasses.

"Where zackly is Stubsterris?" he asked vaguely.

"It's back there," said Fern, pointing behind her. "Quite a long way. We walked for miles and miles, and my feet feel like they're bursting. Are you a fairy?"

Pinch turned to Fern. "Lubkin!" he muttered, rolling his glittering eyes in disgust. "No, I am not a fairy, whatever that is. I am Keeper of the Copse and Boscage Abouts, small snub-nubbed pod of Looey Smurser. And I would thank you to remember as much." He stood up on his branch and raised himself to his full height in an attempt to look dignified.

"We meant no offence, Keeper," said Mack. "We are strangers here and new to the ways of your land. All we want is to find Malvolia Du Mal and . . . "

"A-ha," cried Pinch, his voice taking on a serious and hard edge. "You mean *Queen* Malvolvoleer. She passed by here some time ago with her retinue. You seek an audience with her Lustrousness?"

Mrs Mercer looked anxiously at Jamie, not quite sure of what to say next. Malvolia had wasted no time proclaiming herself the Queen of Mithaca. And it had certainly not taken her long to gather together what Pinch described as her "retinue". Pinch himself seemed to have accepted her quite readily. They would have to be very careful. Pinch might not prove to be the friend and guide that they were looking for after all.

Fern, who only knew an audience from television quiz shows and who had no idea of what a Lustrousness or a Retinue was, sniffed.

"Queen Fat Rubbish," she said, and continued while the others listened in horror. "Queen Soapy-scent Dimmo. She's pinched Karrax and we want to get her for it. And she broke my tooth when I bit her."

There was an uncomfortable silence which lasted for some moments, and then Pinch's face wrinkled into a broad smile and he clapped his hands.

"Well, why didn't you say so before, instead of wasting my time? I thought you might have been her spies. The purdling dimmo . . . heh, I like that word small ugly one called Fern . . . yes, the Dimmo whished through my thicket just before sunrise. All mispy airs and graces she was and full of herself. She smiled a lot but I could tell she was up to no good. Called herself a queen. Why my old man has a better claim. She bid me good-day and wished me long health and she did it all through her teeth as if the words were sticking in her gizzard."

"Just her?" Jamie asked, fearing the worst for Karrax. "She was alone?"

"She was not," said Pinch, hopping off the bough.

"She was squodged in a rough and woody carry-throne affair and had a mimbling swatch of Skoddermen traipsing with her, carrying her and a Childydragger in a cage. It looked sick, it looked very sick, as if it had the sprots or something. I gather that this Karrax is the Chillydrag, your friend."

"Yes," said Fern, upset to think that Karrax was ill.

"The Skoddermen are easy to sway," said Mack, speaking low, almost to himself. "If your will is strong enough they will do anything for you. I . . . " Mack stopped, and Pinch stared at him long and hard.

"At least one of you has been here before then," he said quietly, and then he continued seriously. "What does she want with just that snemming, eh? Cold dragons aren't zackly ten a peggy but why bother to cage and carry that one?"

"He can do something that she can't," said Jamie. "And he could have led her to something that she wants only she doesn't know that Karrax knows where it is, and anyway it isn't where she thinks it is . . . because . . . because we've got it."

"You sound as understandable as Miss Potter explaining maths," said Fern, turning up her nose.

Pinch scratched his head. "I see," he said. "Actually, it all sounds a slodge of wet giffle to me," he admitted. "But I don't doubt that *you* know what you're doing. I wouldn't bother too much about her new Ladyship either. We have ways here of dealing with trimpling upsters, though I hope you do find Queen Whatsernotch, and if you do then I hope you whomp her one from me." He looked them over critically. "It'll take more than the four of you to fodge the Skoddermen, though. They keep emselves to emselves for the most part, but when they's roused and waspish they can be vicious and mean."

"Please, Pinch, which way did she go?" said Mrs Mercer. They had enough to contend with, without dwelling on the thought of what the Skoddermen might do if they ever caught up with them.

"Southish and westaway and a bit to the right," Pinch replied, pointing east. "Leastways, that way, and at a fair treddle for all her flubber. Seems wherever she was going she wanted to get there in a hurry. And there's Skoddermen slubbering from everywhere to be with her."

"What is over there?" asked Jamie.

"Heart's Hill, eventually," said Mack, earning another strange look from Pinch. "She'll be heading for Heart's Hill."

"Aye," Pinch agreed. "Maybe she will. It's where the last one that came and wanted to make us all his slaves and slodges went. Something to do with what's there, you know, or p'raps you don't know, seeing as how you're from Stubsterris." Pinch paused and addressed Mack. "Do I know you, gloomling? I'm sure I know you."

"The children . . . " said Mrs Mercer quickly, noticing Fern yawn, " . . . they've been up all night. Is there anywhere near where we can shelter and rest a little before we carry on?"

Pinch thought for a moment. "Maybe there is," he said. "Maybe there isn't." He folded his arms. "I'm not a Keeper for me good looks alone, Looey Smurser. There's something you're not telling me. I can feel it in my skelebones."

Mrs Mercer bit her lip. "I'm just anxious for the children," she said, truthfully enough. "If there are so many Skoddermen flocking to Malvolia, then it can't be safe to be out and about."

Pinch sniffed. "Jamie's not so bad," he said. "But I can understand you being afeared for the small, simple little podling." He frowned and then nodded his head quickly, as if coming to a sudden decision. "There's Ditching," he said after a moment. "Down the fields and across the stream. You'll find it easily enough. It used to be Old Maudy's cottage but she doesn't use it any longer. There's lots of travellers kip there for a night or two. Long as you keep it clean and replace any firewood you use, you're welcome to it for as long as needs be. And if you do what you came here to do, whatever that is, and if you do happen to come back this way, then call and let me know. I'm always here."

"Can't you come with us?" Jamie asked. "If only to show us the way?"

"Can't," said Pinch, winking. "I'm on guard, remember?"

Mrs Mercer thanked him, Jamie smiled his thanks and Fern blew Pinch a mischievous kiss, which Pinch swatted in the air as if it was something live and nasty like a midge. When Jamie saw Fern take Mack's hand again he thought of something.

"Can I break off a stick?" he asked. "For Mack. It doesn't even have to be a new stick. One of these would do." And he bent down to pick up a thin, small branch from the ground. "He's blind, you see. He— '

There was a crack and Jamie looked up. Pinch had snapped off a cane-thick willow wand with one twist of his wiry little fist. There was a peculiar look in his eyes. Not friendly, not friendly at all, Jamie thought. He stared as Pinch opened his mouth and stripped the willow of its bark with teeth that were white as bone and sharp as needles. He spat out the bark and held out the cane, still wet with green sap.

"Blind, eh?" he whispered, as Jamie took the stick. "With my complibles."

"Thank you," Jamie said. He cast a last glance behind as he caught up with the others. Pinch was staring after them and continued to stare until they dropped from sight.

They crossed the fields, ever watchful for the slightest flash of pink in the distance that would give Malvolia away. Of course, Malvolia had no reason to think that anyone might be following her and she could have stuck to the open and the quickest ways. Yet, even though she now had a pack of Skoddermen, drawn to her like nails to a magnet and bearing the caged Karrax, they saw nothing at all.

They followed Pinch's instructions and after about half an hour came to a small stream that crossed their path in swift shallows over a pebbly river bed. The sun was high in the sky and, after crossing the stream, using the larger pebbles as stepping stones (which took longer than it should since Fern had to direct Mack's feet at every step) they all slumped down on the far bank to rest. It had been slow going with Mack on tow. No one actually said anything, though they realised that in the event of them being spotted by any unfriendly being Mack would stand little chance of flight on his own, and would just hold the others up if they chose to stay with him. Wherever they were going it was going to be a long and difficult journey.

Fern kicked off her shoes and socks and wriggled her hot toes in the cool air. The silver water, sweeping over the pebbly shallows and glinting where the sun struck the edges of its small waves, looked cool and inviting. She wriggled over to the edge of the river and dangled her feet in the water. It was only a short step – or at least a short hop off the river bank – to wading shin-deep in the chilly water. Then Jamie followed, and even Mrs Mercer, with a girlish flick of her head, removed her shoes and started to paddle, shyly at first and then laughing and splashing as much as the children.

The water was icy and the pebbles of the river bed felt ticklish on their feet. It was Fern who started splashing, trying to kick as much water as she could over Jamie, and Jamie, taking advantage of his greater size, gave Fern a shove that sent her sprawling in the water, soaking her from the waist down. When Fern started to use a few choice words Mrs Mercer intervened and decided that, wet or not, it was time to move on to Ditching. They waded to the bank with Fern muttering and trying to kick water down Jamie's back in revenge.

"Where's Mack?" Fern asked, jumping on to the warm grass and squeezing her sodden clothes through her fingers. Mrs Mercer turned around.

"I don't know. He was here a moment ago. At least, I think he was. Mack?" she called tentatively and then more urgently. "Mack!"

"Perhaps he's gone to the toilet," said Fern innocently. "I think *I* want to."

"Mum?" Jamie asked with a sinking feeling in his stomach. "You don't think he's gone because he thought he was holding us back, do you?"

Mrs Mercer searched the river bank with her eyes, not really listening to what Jamie or Fern were saying. "I left it just there," she said, poking in the longer grass with her toes. "I'm sure I left it there." She raised her voice in a shout: "Mack! Where are you? Are you all right? Mack! Can you hear me? Mack!"

It only took Jamie a moment to realise what it was his mother was looking for. He felt as if he was going to be sick. Mack was gone. Mum's bag was gone and, worst of all, the Heart of Mithaca was gone too.

Fern looked wide-eyed and incredulous. Jamie was white with anger. Mrs Mercer stood on the bank, her hands spread in a helpless gesture. They all called at the top of their voices for Mack to come back, heedless of anyone else who might hear, but only the echoes of their cries came back to them over the happy trickling of the stream.

"You were right after all, Jim," said Fern miserably, picking up a rock and flinging it into the water. "Mack's still a baddie, after all . . . "

11
Cabbage and Apple Lollop

Jamie and Fern sat on the soft grass of the river bank, staring into the clear waters. Mrs Mercer continued to hunt through the bushes and the tall weeds in a rather desperate way, but found nothing. She came back to where the children sat and looked every bit as miserable as they did. Only Fern found it hard to believe what the others knew to be true. Mack had gone and he had taken the Heart with him.

At the moment when their spirits were at their lowest there was a rustle in the bushes by the bank and a small figure stepped out. Pinch's scowling eyes took in the situation straight away and he said in a sour voice, "I knew I knew the gloomling lubbock. I knew I knew him when Jamie said he was blind. I says to myself, sat sitting there, I know that gargaloom. My old dadder told me all about the scagger. Oh, he called himself Mack he did, but I knew him. He's called McGee." Pinch spat on the ground. "The treacherous gorn skebbin."

"We know what he's called," said Jamie.

"He's our friend," said Fern bravely, earning herself a snort from Pinch.

"Oh, is that so?" he said. "Well, did you know that your so-called friend once— "

"We know," said Jamie. "We know everything. But he

said that he'd changed and we decided to trust him. We really didn't think that he would . . . " and he faltered, unable to say the words "betray us".

"Still," said Pinch, with a wry smile. "Look on the bridely side. An old lubbage bag ain't nothing to winge and frowndle over." As he drew nearer he noticed the desolate expression on Mrs Mercer's face. "Or is there some more to it than that, eh, Looey Smurser? Is this the something that you was keeping back from old Pinch, eh? Was I right to leave my post and come whishling down? What else 'septing grubbage was in the bag? Gold, p'raps? Summing rarey?"

"Not gold, Pinch," said Mrs Mercer. "Something more precious than that."

"Everything's up and down," said Fern, who was confused, angry and sad. "First there's Karrax, then there isn't. Then there's Mack, and then there isn't. Then there's the Heart and then there's nothing. I wish we'd never come to this rotten hole. This is supposed to be a nice place. Where are the unicorns and the elves and the dragons that Mack promised us would be here? Or was he tricking us about those too?"

Jamie put his arm about Fern and, this time, Fern didn't wriggle away but sat still, staring into the water. Pinch blew out his cheeks.

" 'First there's the *Heart*'?" he repeated, deadly serious. "Now then, if you're not just chatling about any old heart then you can only mean the one thing when you say that, podling Fern." Pinch went and sat down by Mrs Mercer and stared at her. "I think you'd best tell me everything, Looey Smurser, every last bellady detail, and no holding back this time, and then, well, we'll see what can be done." And, while Jamie still held Fern close, Mrs Mercer told Pinch everything, about Karrax, about the Heart, about Mack, every last bellady detail.

Pinch listened patiently. Jamie heard the words that his mother was saying, and he heard Pinch tut and groan, obviously aware of the true seriousness of the situation. But to Jamie it was as if he was listening to a story, a wild and fantastic story that had taken a bitter turn in the telling. He stared into the water that flowed past them. Fern must have felt something similar too because she whispered: "I want to go home, Jim. I want to wake up and go home."

"You said it yourself, Fern," Jamie replied. "You can only wake up from dreams. This is no dream."

Perhaps for the first time Jamie sympathised with Fern. The scruffy house in Stubbs Terrace seemed almost desirable, but there was no means of going back there, not without Karrax and certainly not without the Heart.

Behind Jamie, Pinch was pacing the bank, hands behind his back, in deep thought. Mrs Mercer sat with her arms about her knees, staring down-river.

"I don't know," said Pinch gloomily, as if in answer to an unspoken question. "I just don't know. It's bad, it's whomping bad. It's worse than the last time." He turned on Mrs Mercer. "What you want to carry the rarey old Heart round in a skiffy bag for eh, Looey Smurser? And what you want to go and tell that gloomling skebbin about it for? Never trust a snitchling twice is what my old dad used to say."

"Pinch," said Jamie turning round. "Mum feels bad enough about it as it is. We all do. We thought that Mack was honest, despite what he did in the past. But it's no good blaming anybody. We have to do something."

"Besides," said Fern, close to tears, "you didn't

seem specially bothered by Malvolia when she first arrived, and she was going off to find the Heart where she thinks it is, only it isn't, so I don't see what the fuss is about. Mack's just, just probably borrowed the Heart, that's all, just to keep it safe. He'll come back. I know he will!"

"Tchah!" said Pinch. "Mebbe, podling. Though I shouldn't go holding your breath and counting to ninetyleven while you're waiting. No, there's things to be done," he said decisively. "Folks to tell and places to be got ready, and standing about here and pulling each other to dribs and tetters isn't going to help." Pinch made some calculations on his fingers, counting until he was satisfied he had all the sums right.

"Listen, all of you listen!" Jamie and Fern turned round and Mrs Mercer tilted her head. "Movolvolilly Dum Wossnim is smiddling about on foot and it'll take her a fewanabit days to get to Heart's Hill even if her Skoddermen carry her all the way. The snitchling McGloomling *has* to take that much longer 'cause his eyes is out. Though . . . " Pinch paused a second, "if he has the Heart, it might just sniff out the way for him." He waved a hand. "No matter, either way we have time to get things ready, and enough time p'raps to get things finished."

Pinch looked at Mrs Mercer and the children as if he expected them to know what to do next. Pinch puffed out his cheeks, exasperated.

"The stedgy would-be Queen Whatserflubber and the gloomling feggerspilth McGee are both heading for the same place with the same thought in their heads, yes?"

"Heart's Hill, you mean?" said Mrs Mercer. Pinch nodded his head eagerly.

"Zackly. It's where she thinks the Heart is and the best place of all to get what she wants. Well, I might not have much brinnage up-top, but it strikes me that the thing to do is to get our own army and whallop on to Heart's Hill before they both do and surprise and trodge 'em afore they trodges us."

Jamie tried to smile. Of course that was the answer. But, like the answer to a lot of problems, it was easier to say than do. Fern looked with admiration at the little man. There was nothing she would love more right at that moment than to trodge Malvolia.

"Yes," she said. "That's what we'll do!"

Mrs Mercer bowed her head to Pinch in a small gesture of thanks. "The only trouble is, Pinch," she said, "we could never hope to make up enough time as it is, let alone take more to get an army together. We don't know anyone here and I wouldn't even know how to go about raising an army."

Pinch looked crest-fallen hearing those words.

"Oh, Looey Smurser," he said, tutting. "What you want to go and squish the kidlings' hopes for, eh? Haven't you no dash and daring left in your spiridge? Haven't you no spiddle to splot in the eye o' bad luck and make it blink? I thought you was turnling good grit. You just going to sit there then and mizzle and mopse and feel sorry for yourself?" He winked at the children while he was talking and they felt better, though neither could say why. Perhaps it was the way their mother suddenly hung her head, like a little schoolgirl being ticked off for not taking part in the games.

"You know me, don't yer!" said Pinch. "And when the rest of the good folk about here realise what's happened, why, they'll come a-running. There's ways of getting in touch with them. Fast ways that not even Movovervile and Mcgiffle know about."

"Blast you!" cried Mrs Mercer, with fire in her eyes. "You're right. We came to finish her off and we *will*. And we'll start now by— "

"We'll start now by going to Ditching and resting," said Pinch, with an air of authority in his gravelly voice. "The kidlings can kip a snatch, and you can light a fire and stew whatever grubbage you find in Old Maudy's hudge. And I – well, I've places to go to and calls to make and things to see. Now, off we go to Ditching, and you, buggly grub," he addressed Fern. "You *can* carry me now. My feetlers is hot and boshed . . . "

The small cottage called Ditching was run-down and overgrown, but its timbers and thatch were sound enough. It lay in a small hollow some half a mile from the stream. There had been a small garden there too at one time, and an orchard which sported a few green apples, not quite ripe but fine for cooking. There was a well with clear water, and inside the house (which was surprisingly clean) Mrs Mercer found pans on a wood-burning stove, kindling, and half a side of salt pork hung in a tiny cool-room over an underground spring. Fern shook down apples, Jamie rooted up some young cabbages that had seeded themselves from last year, and Mrs Mercer lit the wood-stove with kindling and tinder – which took her a while until Pinch showed her how it was done – and hacked off slices of pork with an old kitchen knife and set them to boil with the cabbage.

Pinch sniffed the aroma from the pans and nodded, approvingly. "Boiled pork, gribbage and apple lollop," he said. "You'd best save me some for when I get back." And, before anyone could ask where he was going, he sprang out of the house, and was gone.

"Do you think Pinch can really do anything?" Jamie asked, trying his best to peel the apples with the dull knife.

"'Course he can," said Fern, springing to the little man's defence. "You just have to trust him."

"We trusted Mack, didn't we?" said Jamie. "And look what happened. He used us to get what he wanted and then he left us. I hate him."

Mrs Mercer came over to Jamie and said quietly, "Enough now."

"But it's true, Mum," Jamie whispered back. "We were stupid to think that he'd ever change. I despise him."

"It's Fern I'm thinking of," said Mrs Mercer. "Now scout about and find some plates."

Jamie rooted in a cupboard and brought out wooden platters, but there were no forks so they all had to eat with their fingers, much to Fern's delight. She even forgot that she didn't like cabbage and stuffed her mouth full of it. When the platters were wiped clean Mrs Mercer doled out boiled apples, sweetened with crusty honey from a half-full stone jar.

Fern managed only a little of hers before her fingers became unbearably sticky and she ran out to wash them in the stream. Jamie and his mother finished the rest of their apple lollop in silence. Mrs Mercer had only just started to gather up the platters when the door burst open and Fern stood there panting and gasping for breath.

"Mum! M-mum!" she stammered. "Outside, quick! Th-there's something, s-s-something you should see."

Mrs Mercer leapt to her feet and ran to the door. Jamie's nostrils tickled with a smell of burning. "We're surrounded," he thought, panic rising. "Malvolia has come back with the Skoddermen and they've set light to the thatch. They're going to burn us alive!"

"Jamie," said Mrs Mercer, breathlessly. "Come and see!"

While they had been eating, three dragons had winged their way silently and stealthily into the garden at Ditching Hollow. Firewurms they were and their vast bodies, armoured with golden scales, cast huge shadows. Their heads were horned, three horns to each head Jamie noted, and their black, polished beaks were curved like that of an eagle. As they reared, huge and soundless, their small forelegs beat the air in time with the massive wings, whose membranes filtered the sunlight's yellow fire. They rested on their powerful haunches, their feet taloned with claws as thick as drain-pipes that tapered to needle points. All around, smoke curled and billowed from their nostrils, a visible sign of the furnaces that burned within, and in their eyes, faceted like Karrax's (only these were red as new blood), blazed a light that nearly blinded. From behind each rose a tail, tall and strong, tipped with a midnight-blue arrow-head of leathery flesh.

And from the back of the foremost, the largest of them all, a gravelly voice cried: "Whishling, wizzling flight to wherever we want to go. Not bad, kidlings and Looey Smurser, eh? Not bad!"

12

Dragonstone and Leestone

The dragons loomed so large in the clearing that Pinch was little more than a wart on their gleaming backs. Jamie stood with one hand upon the door post, his other hand to his open mouth as if he were trying to cover a cry of fear or perhaps a whoop of joy. Dragons! Fire-breathing, winged and terrible! And Pinch was actually riding one!

Fern crept up behind him, and over both their heads Mrs Mercer stared in awe herself. The dragon that carried Pinch lifted its broad tail, on to which Pinch hopped and was lowered to the ground. He stood with a broad grin on his face and a sparkle in his eyes, as if to say, "There now. What do you think of that?" What he actually said was, "Any lollop left?"

The Mercers backed away from the doorway. The dragons remained in the garden while Pinch went into the house. He hardly said a word as he ate all that was left of the stewed apple and honey, before starting on the cabbage and ham. Fern stood at the small window gazing out.

Pinch finished eating and licked his lips. "Mickling good grubbage," he said appreciatively. "I thought we'd start with the dragons, you know, before the others. They're the biggest and the bestest and gentlest, you see, and I thought that if I could get two or three of them to listen, then the rest of Mithaca would follow sure as fleggs is fleggs."

"Gentlest?" Jamie cried. If the great beasts outside were the gentlest things that they would meet then what else lay before them?

"Aye," Pinch said. "Oh, not that they couldn't melt a mountain into slodge if they had a mind. Trouble is they don't do anything unless they're prodged. And it takes a lot to prodge a dragon."

"Where – where did you find them?" Mrs Mercer asked.

"Find 'em?" Pinch said. "Find 'em? Who said they was lost? T'isn't the sort of thing you trip over, Looey Smurser. I didn't find 'em. You might say they found me. Leastways, those three Hurglings came when I called."

"How?" said Jamie. "How did you call them?"

Pinch looked at him with one eyebrow raised. "I ain't the Keeper of the Copse and Boscage Abouts for nothing, you know. You call dragons at a Dragonstone. There's one just a-down the hill in a willowithy thickage. More often than not they ignores ordinary folk, though they respects a Keeper. Shosh, I thought everybody knew that. Dragonstones is reserved for dragons, though. Folks that need to talk to other folks just use the other stones." Pinch saw the blank looks he was getting.

"You know, like the Leestone at Ember. It's where we're going, just as soon as I've kipped, to get some more bodies on our side, as it were. Have to keep your strength up." And, without another word, he jumped down from the table and threw himself into a pile of bracken in the corner and shut his eyes.

"How can he sleep at a time like this?" Jamie thought, and then he too yawned. He glanced at the window where Fern still stood. There was an intense look on Fern's face, a look of deep concentration that Jamie had never seen before, as if Fern were straining her ears to catch the sound of a distant music that was lovely but unclear. Mrs Mercer also noticed Fern's expression.

"Fern?" she called. "Fern, come away from the window. They might not like to be stared at so."

"They don't mind," said Fern, in a wistful voice. "Timbar doesn't mind anyway. He likes to be stared at. He thinks it means people like him."

Jamie yawned again and twisted a finger at his temple. Mrs Mercer smiled and then went over to Fern and placed her hands on her daughter's shoulders. The dragons were at rest now, their huge feet firmly planted on the ground, their wings folded at their backs. Faint wisps of dark smoke curled from the small nostrils in their beaks.

"Which one is Timbar?" Mrs Mercer whispered. Fern pointed a finger at the largest, most magnificent beast. Its eyes were half closed and directed at the little window, and it moved its head slowly, as if in greeting.

"That's him," Fern said. "It's not his real name, only the bit of it that I could remember after he'd said it. The others are Rima, that's the one with the greyest beak, and Venior, he's the one with the broken third horn. That's what they said." She paused and frowned. "Actually I don't mean 'said'. I mean sang, I think. Like music, but you can't hear it, you just feel it in your head and it isn't really like music – it's sort of waves, but they all mean something. Do you know what I mean? Can't you hear it too?"

Mrs Mercer couldn't hear the fire-dragons' song but she understood what Fern meant. She recalled the time when she had first heard Karrax speak to her. Karrax's voice – if the sensation she had felt in her mind could be called something so commonplace as a voice – had sounded high and sharp and clear, and even though the great dragons would have had a different song, Mrs Mercer had some idea of what Fern must have been hearing.

Jamie sat at the table with his head propped in his hands, suddenly so tired that he only half heard what his mother and Fern were saying. Even so, it was enough to make him feel a little out of things. Mrs Mercer had been able to understand Karrax and now Fern, it appeared, could hear the great fire-dragons. Jamie listened through his tiredness, and heard nothing except Pinch's soft snores from the corner and his mother and Fern's low whispers. He crept over to where Pinch lay and dropped down beside the little man.

So much was happening; so many important things were bound to happen. Jamie wanted to stay awake, afraid that if he slept the world they were in would change when next he woke. He might sleep and wake to find that Mack had used the Heart to succeed where he had failed before. Jamie was even half afraid that he would wake to the walls of his own bedroom in the house at Stubbs Terrace. He reached out a finger and brushed Pinch's dry, old face and made him mumble in his sleep. Jamie's eyelids felt heavy, his thoughts started to wander on nothing in particular, and he slept, while Fern talked to dragons.

"They don't really know what's going on," said Fern. "Pinch has told them that the whole of Mithaca is in danger, like last time, and they don't really want to fight, but they say they will if they have to. They're very old, older than you, Mum, older than the trees out there." Fern's eyes widened, suddenly catching a dragon-thought. "They're older than nearly everything, older than the hills, as old as the rocks. They say – they're almost as old as the Starchild even, because they were the Starchild's first thought." Fern looked at her mother. "What's the Starchild, Mum?"

Mrs Mercer said she didn't know. "What else do they say?" she asked, gazing at the great beasts with the eyes of a wondering child.

"Nothing much really," said Fern. "They're nervous. They can feel that something tremendous is about to happen, they say that they can smell it on the wind and see it in the stars." Fern yawned, a great, sleepy yawn. Mrs Mercer lifted her from the window and carried her to where Jamie lay, and where there was still room for another tired head on the bracken. Talking to dragons was hard work and Fern's eyes closed at once.

Mrs Mercer stood watching her children and Pinch for a long time. She was wary of sleeping, but then, she told herself, what harm could come to them with such guardians on the doorstep? She settled herself at the table and laid her head on her arm. Pinch was right, they ought to keep their strength up. There was no telling what lay ahead.

Pinch was the first to wake some hours later. It was dusky in the little cottage and the last few rays of the sun shone through the dusty window. He stretched and squeezed himself out from under Fern, who had rolled over on him in her sleep. After checking that the dragons were still outside, he woke Mrs Mercer.

"We must be going," he said. "It's not far to the

nearest Leestone, but you and your kidlings have never stridden a Hurgling afore, and there's a bit of a knack to it." Mrs Mercer shook herself, eased the crick out of her neck and roused Jamie first. Fern woke to the sound of the others moving, and stood groggily.

The dragons were waiting patiently in the garden, their wings at rest, but they roused themselves at the sight of the four figures that came out of Ditching in the gloom. Pinch looked at them and scratched his head.

"Whoo, hadn't thought of this," he muttered.

"Thought of what?" said Mrs Mercer.

"Well," said Pinch a little embarrassed. "Talking to dragons is all very well when you does it through a Dragonstone. Then they understands. That's how I telled 'em to pick me up and fetch me here. Trouble is, how do I get it through to these Hurgleys now that we want to be up and gone to raise the others, eh?"

Fern knew, of course, and explained as much to Pinch's utter astonishment. "A podling!" he cried. "Talking to Flemmings without a Dragonstone? Shosh, would you believe it? Mind you, if your great-gone-grandferdaddy was from hereabouts that might explain it, eh? Okee-Dogey, Fernling, hexercise this grandly talent and tell them we want to go to the Leestone at Ember." He added finally, " 'Tain't the best Stone abouts, but it's the nearest and we'll get through to enough as makes no odds."

Fern walked over and touched Timbar's scaled flank. The great dragon bent its head and looked down at her. "Pinch says we have to go to the Leestone at Ember, please," she said.

Pinch puffed his cheeks. "Could have done that myself," he said, unimpressed. "They don't speak Stubbsterrish. They won't know what you're saying. They— "

"It isn't what you say," said Fern. "It's *how* you say it." She touched her forehead. "In here. You just think it and they know. See!"

Timbar lowered his heavy tail until the broad tip was flat on the ground. "You have to stand on that, Mum," said Fern. "And Timbar will lift you on. There's no other way, not unless you've got a long ladder."

There was a debate then as to who should ride with whom and on which dragon, and it was finally decided that Mrs Mercer would ride with Fern on Timbar, that Pinch should take the smaller Rima, and that Jamie should have Venior all to himself. Mrs Mercer and Fern stood on the tip of Timbar's tail and held each other as they were lifted slowly on to his back.

"There's a saddle-like scatch-scale," Pinch called, watching them scrabble on to the dragon's back. "Put your botches on that and grip tight with your kneebones. And grab hold of the wartish bits behind where their ears should be. That's it." He turned to Jamie and smiled. "Now you, Jamie Mercer."

Venior's tail lay on the ground and, almost as soon as his feet touched it, Jamie was whisked into the air and deposited on the dragon's back. He found the long tendrils of hard flesh that grew from the back of Venior's horns and clung on, settling himself as comfortably as he could, his heart pounding, twenty feet from the ground, while Pinch mounted Rima. Venior felt cold to the touch, which Jamie found surprising.

The sun set behind the far hills in a bright wash of yellow and rose, flooding the western sky that was already picked out with a few early stars between small, scudding clouds.

"Well?" Pinch cried, sounding a little pompous now

that he was astride a dragon. "What you waiting for, podling? Tell 'em to fly."

Fern, sitting a little awkwardly in front of Mrs Mercer, laid a hand on Timbar's head.

"We're ready, Timbar," she said.

The great dragon's wings uncurled slowly from its back and stretched to their full extent, slightly raised to avoid the unfurling wings of Rima and Venior. There was a barely audible thwack of leathery wings against the still air and a sudden lift that left Jamie's stomach feeling as if it had been dropped behind in the garden at Ditching, and they were up. The garden, the surrounding orchard, the house itself, receded into the deepening night as the dragons took to the air. Jamie clung as tightly as he could without feeling that he was hurting his dragon and he swayed a little as Venior steadied on the wing.

"Hang on, skimpling," Pinch called. "We're off!"

Jamie felt his stomach lurch again as the dragons shifted from upward to forward flight, and the air whistled past his ears and billowed his shirt. He would have closed his eyes only he had no intention of missing one second of this ride. He might never, ever be able to tell anyone of it (if ever they returned home) but he wanted to fix the joy and the wonder and the magic of it in his heart for all time. He was riding a dragon! A living, breathing, burning, airborne, fiery battleship of another world. He felt the powerful muscles beneath him contract and expand as Venior's wings rose and fell, lifting them higher the further they flew. He felt the hard scales at his knees, sharp and unyielding, as his feet found a foothold between them. He opened his mouth and almost lost his breath as Venior gathered speed, hurtling through the air like a smoking arrow, chasing his brothers.

Mithaca dissolved into a dark grey tapestry of field and forest. "This," Jamie thought, "this is what you'd see through the window of an aeroplane." And, as the air rushed by him and as Venior buffeted on a rising current of warm air, he thought, "But you'd never feel this. Not this much fright and glory."

He stared ahead at the horizon where the sun was dipping the last arc of its golden head below the black hills. Out of the corner of his eye he caught the pale moon to the left, borrowing the dying light of the sun. Jamie shut his eyes and gave himself over to the feel of flight and, almost as soon as he did, it was over. The dragons swooped and fell and beat their wings to halt their flight, alighting on a low hill that was swathed in moonlight and shadows.

"Ember," said Pinch's voice out of the darkness. Jamie stayed on Venior's back, feeling the dragon's muscles rise and fall. He looked right and left. The black shadows of Timbar and Rima loomed against the purple sky. In front of them, the tall, dark shadow of a standing stone reared against the heavens.

"And that black grannidge, poking at the welkin, is the Leestone. Pish!" hissed Pinch, from somewhere in the darkness. "I forgot about torches. Podling?"

Jamie heard Fern call out to his left.

"Get the Hurgling to flare, will you?" Pinch cried. "Just a middling flame to light the way, so's I don't trip and squidge this old skull on the Leestone."

A second later there was a bright flash of light as Timbar, at Fern's request, sent a column of bright flame into the night sky, maintaining his fire so that they might see where they were.

By the yellow light of Timbar's fire, Pinch strode forward and placed his small hands on the tall column of stone that grew out of the ground. He gripped the rock at its base and pressed his forehead to it, mumbling something strange from his lips as he did so. For some moments there was nothing, no noise, only the gentle roar of Timbar's flame as it burned, and then, slowly, surely, a silver light was kindled at the base of the rock. Pale lines slithered about the stone, rising like snakes, and there was a crackle in the air like the sound of pylons on a hot, humid day.

"This is it," Jamie thought, twisting Venior's rein-like tendrils around his wrists.

The crackle grew to a rumble like thunder. It shook the ground and shivered the Leestone. Pinch, summoning all the strength he had, poured his thought into the stone, sweating and trembling as he summoned Mithaca to their aid.

13

The Borderers

Fern watched the pale lines crawl about the surface of the Leestone, widening until they met in one brilliance that was brighter than Timbar's flame. As the dragon's fire died away, and the hilltop at Ember was lit by the light from the stone itself, she whispered, "What's he doing, Mum?"

"This must be the way to get in touch with the others," Mrs Mercer guessed. "There are probably other stones like this all over Mithaca."

As she spoke, the noise from the Leestone dropped to a low hum, like an idling engine, and its light throbbed.

"Like telephone boxes," Jamie said. "Or like a fire alarm or something, telling everyone to get ready and be on their guard."

The humming of the Leestone strengthened in one last, brief burst and Pinch's figure, his head still pressed to the stone, was little more than a black shadow against the pulsating white light. Gradually the noise abated and the light faded as the silence came.

"What now?" Jamie asked the darkness.

"We wait," said Pinch. He sounded weary, as if using the stone had drained him. "We wait for those who have heard to come. Don't know how long."

From behind black clouds the moon sailed out and shone down on the hill, and by its watery light Pinch gathered sticks and kindling to make a small fire a little way from the Leestone, which a gentle jet of flame from Rima soon had crackling away. Mrs Mercer and Fern dismounted from Timbar and crept to the fire. Jamie waited a while, staring from Venior's back away into the black night.

"Who *will* come?" he asked, descending a little shakily on Venior's tail, which the great dragon flicked up when he started to try and slide down himself.

"Hard to say," Pinch admitted, flinging a stick on the fire, watching it catch light and snap. Jamie knew that Pinch was in no mood for talk after his effort at the Leestone, but he had to know.

"Well," he persisted. "What happened last time, you know, when Mack—?"

Pinch looked up sharply. The firelight, flickering in his large eyes, gave him a devilish appearance.

"I was younger then," he said quietly. "I only knows what my old dad told me afterwards. I wasn't no part of the war then. I had other things on my plate, but my old dad went to fight, him and his brother, my uncle Tacker. I don't think folks properly understood the danger they were in. I don't think folks do until it's nearly too late, skimpling. I only hope that there's enough left with long enough memories to remember and understand it now." Pinch paused. "Now it's happening all over again, and this time old Pinch is right in the thick of it. Who'd have thought that, eh? Certainly not my old dad, rest his old boots and bones."

"But didn't you have battles and things before Mack came the first time?" Jamie asked. "We do, all the time. Every day there's somebody fighting somebody else, though I don't really know why. It's mostly over land and religion, I think."

"Maybe that's so, where you come from," Pinch said. "Stubsterris sounds a doomly place, specially the Lidgeon. Here, it's not like that. Oh, there's arguments and quabbles, s'only natural and proper, folks being folks, but there's nobody ever killed another body just a'cause they fell out over a bit o' land. And there's nobody ever thought he was that good and better than anyone else that he could order them about, not Skoddermen, not Trolls, not Troggs nor Toad-whimps neither. Not even Murglings, and they's the worst of all, so my old dad used to say."

"And don't you have a king or a queen?" Jamie asked. "We do, and princesses and princes."

"If we do have prissies and prissenses, *I* don't know about it," Pinch said. "There *was* the Starchild, but that was longer ago than there's any to remember, and he hain't been seen for mountains' years . . . Whish! What was that?"

Pinch cocked his head, listening. From somewhere out of the darkness beyond the small campfire came the sound of hooves. It was hard to tell how many, but Pinch's trained ears knew. He stiffened all over. "Two horses," he whispered. "Let's hope that it's just the first of many."

The Mercers huddled together as the cantering drew nearer. To their left and from the dim shadows of the slope of the hill a man's voice called out: "Would it be ye has summoned the Borderers?"

Pinch stood up and returned the call.

"Aye, it is the Keeper of the Copse and Boscage Abouts. I called through the Stone for any of stout heart to come to the aid of the world we know."

It was a formal greeting, and Pinch stood with a hand raised, saluting the darkness. There were low mutters and then the horses and riders cantered forward into the small circle of light – a man and a woman, dressed in dark colours. Their heads were bare and their hair, long and yellow, fell about their shoulders. The man had a beard, though his face was still young and both he and the woman had the same dark eyes. As they drew nearer Jamie saw that a bow and a quiver of white-feathered arrows were slung at each saddle.

The riders dismounted and strode forward. They didn't seem at all surprised to see the three dragons sitting like statues beyond the campfire.

"Greetings," said the young man, addressing Pinch alone. "I am Edwyn and this is my sister Licia. We are Borderers of the Westmarch and we heard your call at Backstone yonder and came with all speed. Your summons was unclear but we understood its urgency, Keeper."

Pinch made a great formal show of thanking the newcomers and he introduced Mrs Mercer, Jamie and Fern properly and seriously and with none of his odd phrasing. He told Edwyn and Licia about Mack and Malvolia and the stolen Heart. The Borderers listened with grave faces. Mrs Mercer sat blushing in the firelight when Pinch got to the point at which Mack disappeared with her bag. Pinch was too kind-hearted to lay the blame on any one person, but Jamie watched his mother shift uncomfortably and stare at the fire. Edwyn and Licia, their dark eyes flashing around the assembled company, made no comments when Pinch had done. Licia ran a hand through her golden hair.

"It explains why the Skoddermen are abroad in numbers," she said, her voice high and sweet as a singer's. "We have spied many different groups of them since yesternoon. They headed east. And, though we ourselves were not challenged, most were armed with clubs and staves, and some had long knives at their belts. We could not see their faces for their hoods were drawn against a light they have no liking for, yet they made great speed as they travelled, as if there was but the one thought in their minds."

"Are we but the six and the Werrym?" Edwyn asked, pointing at this last word to the dragons, looming large in patient attendance in the shadows.

"For the moment," said Pinch. "But if you heard the summons then others will have too. I hope."

"And what plan have ye?" Licia asked, barely glancing at Mrs Mercer and the children.

"Plan?" said Pinch, surprised at being asked. "Well, I thought that we should, well, just trodge 'em, with as many as we can get together."

Licia and Edwyn exchanged looks and smiled.

"Would that all battles were so simple, small warrior," said Edwyn. Jamie frowned at what he thought was the haughty way that Edwyn dismissed Pinch's suggestion.

"Have you ever fought then?" he asked defensively. Edwyn's smile faded and he shook his head.

"Nay, young master. And I have no wish to. But like any right man and true I will if there be just cause. The arrows we carry and the strung bows are not for sport. I was not dismissing the Keeper's plan out of hand. I caution 'gainst haste."

"There's not that much time you know, until Malvolia gets to Heart's Hill," said Fern. "Can't we all fly off now on the dragons and you shoot her with your bow and arrow? She'd do the same to you, you know, if she could."

"Far better we slew the treacherous wizard and restored the Heart to safe-keeping," said Licia, coldly. "The witch Malvolia has broken no laws yet, has harmed no one. We have only your word that she intends harm now, though her assembling the Skoddermen does not bode well; while the wizard McGee holds the means to bring us all to ruin, and has proven to be false in the past." She saw the look of alarm cross the children's faces at the thought that Mack would be shot down. Fern decided there and then that she didn't like the frosty Licia one bit.

"We are telling the truth about Malvolia," said Mrs Mercer. "And doesn't kidnapping Karrax count for anything? You heard Pinch say that she has already proclaimed herself Queen of Mithaca."

"We do not know," said Edwyn, "that the Akhildrakor – forgive me, the Chilldrake – we do not know for sure that it *is* endangered. We do not disbelieve you, and we do not underestimate the graveness of the matter of Malvolia's pretence to rule us. But, when my sister says that t'were best to slay the wizard, she is right. That is what we *should* do, if we were cold and heartless enough to. It is not our way. It was not the way of our fathers before us," said Edwyn. He turned and scanned the night with his dark eyes. "My night-sight is keen, Keeper," he said. "Yet I see none hurry to the Leestone. How long do you think to wait?"

Pinch shrugged his small shoulders. He had expected a host of folk to be there by now, or at least on their way to the Leestone, and he had no other plan than to await for the Mithacans to rise to his call. He sighed; he had thought it would all be so easy.

"*We* shall ride then," said Edwyn, springing to his horse. "And assemble what force we may. You have the word of the Borderers of Westmarch that, even if we persuade none to follow us, at least my sister and I shall meet you at Heart's Hill and lend what strength we may. Farewell, Keeper, until then." He spurred his horse a little way off, waiting for his sister. Licia reached into her belt and drew forth a small knife, which she handed to Mrs Mercer, hilt first.

" 'Tis best a woman arms herself with some means of defence," she said with a slight, friendly smile. "The Fiorwerrym are mighty beasts but there is naught more comforting than the true weight of cold steel."

Mrs Mercer reached out nervously for the dagger. "Thank you, Licia," she said. "I hope I won't need it, but thank you. And thank you for helping us."

" 'Tis ourselves we aid, *if* all you say be true," said Licia, and with a toss of her golden hair she mounted her horse and rode away with Edwyn into the night.

"I don't like her," said Fern, after the sound of hoofs had died away. "She's too frosty and big-headed. Can I see the dagger? And what's a Borderer anyway?"

Mrs Mercer slipped the weapon into her own pocket.

"Borderers is what they sound like," said Pinch. "They watch for trouble on the Borders. Edwyn and Licia are from the Westmarch troop. That's that way." Pinch pointed South. "Then there's Northriddens, Eastfold and Southolm," he added, waving an arm in various directions. "They's trained to fight and fedge with flights and fists," he added, sounding like a shaken lemonade bottle.

Mrs Mercer frowned. "Is it worth waiting any longer?" she asked Pinch. "I feel we're wasting time. Maybe we should get to Heart's Hill as quickly as we can and wait for what assistance the Borderers can find."

Pinch looked miserable. "I felt sure that others would

come," he said. "P'raps I'll just try the Leestone again." Pinch bit his lip in doubtful thought, and wandered over to touch the stone. He was about to press his head to the cold rock when Jamie gave a sudden cry.

"Pinch, there *is* someone over there, look."

Pinch spun round with hope in his eyes and stared where Jamie pointed. He could make out a tall dark shape at the brow of the hill. The figure was motionless but, as he watched, it was joined by a second and then a third. All three stood as silent as they had arrived, pools of dark against the blacker night sky.

"Hail and welcome," Pinch called. "Did you hear my call, or did you just meet with the Borderers?"

The three figures said nothing and moved no nearer. Jamie tried to make out exactly who or what they were, but the fire was between him and them and it was hard to see properly. Then he heard a soft noise at his back and he turned to see yet another tall shape. For a moment his heart skipped a beat. The long dark silhouette reminded him of . . .

"Mack?" he whispered. "Is that you, Mack?" That figure, too, stayed outside the firelight and in the shadows. Mrs Mercer felt uneasy. If these were friends come at Pinch's summons then why did they say nothing? Why did they stand there, threatening them with their silence? She felt a little thrill of menace prickle the hairs on her head.

"Pinch," she called. "I don't think they are here to help." But Pinch had already had the same thought. He skipped away from the Leestone and came closer to the fire. He caught sight of the figure behind Jamie, and another two that no one had noticed at Mrs Mercer's back. Mrs Mercer held Fern to her and reached out for Jamie.

"He said hail," Fern shouted. "Why don't you say something? It's very rude, you know, to stand there and say nothing."

Mrs Mercer pressed a finger to Fern's lips to quieten her, pulling Jamie closer at the same time. Pinch reached into the edge of the fire and pulled out a burning stick which flamed like a little torch.

"Who are you?" he cried, advancing a step or two towards the first group of three figures. He held the burning brand before him, both as a light and a weapon, and as he waved it the dark group retreated slightly down the slope.

"I don't like it," said Fern. "Why don't they speak?"

Mrs Mercer stroked Fern's hair. "They're probably just as scared of us as we are of them. Maybe . . . maybe they're frightened of the dragons," she said, though she didn't believe that for one moment. She fumbled in her pocket and her fingers closed against the cold hardness of Licia's knife. Praying that she wouldn't have to use it, she pulled it out and gripped it tightly without letting the children see what she had done.

"For the third and last time," Pinch called. "Step forward and make yourselves known if you are friends. If you are not friends then I would thank you to be gone with all speed. Here there be dragons."

Fern felt small ripples of Timbar's thought flit through her mind and she shut her eyes to concentrate.

"Pinch," she said. "Timbar can see them."

As Fern spoke the Firewurms shifted uneasily and lowered their tails. Jamie peered through the shadows. More figures had arrived; there were perhaps ten or twelve now, and all stood silent and motionless outside the circle of firelight. Pinch threw down the burning stick.

“What does he say they are, podling?” Pinch asked, trying not to sound alarmed, but when Fern answered, his knees felt weak and his heart began to thump.

“Murglings,” Fern said. “Timbar says they’re Murglings.”

14

Murglings

Slowly, very slowly, Mrs Mercer stood up and pulled Jamie and Fern to their feet. She moved away from the fire and inched over to where the dragons waited. Pinch stood transfixed.

"After all these years of only hearing about you gutter-rots in stories," he was muttering to himself. "Murglings at last, and me without so much as a stick to trodge 'em. Just what would my old dad say, eh?"

"Never mind your old dad," said Fern. "Just get up on Rima and let's be gone."

"Yes, please," said Mrs Mercer, desperately trying not to let the fear she felt creep into her voice. "Please, Pinch. Let's go before there's any trouble." She edged closer to where Timbar's and Venior's tails lay side by side on the ground. Even the knife in her hand seemed little comfort when they were surrounded by so many.

"But where've they come from, eh, Looey Smurser?" Pinch murmured as if in a daze. "They's only legends and hearth-tales. They's only boogey-men and shadders. I dursn't argues against old Timbar and what he says but . . . Murglings! Shoosh!"

"Pinch!" Jamie cried, placing one foot on to Venior's broad tail. "Come on. You'll have us all killed. It's obvious that they've come to be with Malvolia."

"Have they now?" said Pinch, a careless, faraway note in his voice. "Well, well. Would you listen to that now?"

Despite his fear, Jamie listened. At his side, Timbar lifted Mrs Mercer and Fern on to his back and began to unfold his wings.

"Jamie," Fern called in a small, frightened voice. "Timbar says they've come for you. *You* Jamie! Oh, get on Venior quick! Quick, quick!"

Timbar was rising already and Mrs Mercer yelled urgently at Fern to tell him to wait. She had seen the dark figures move nearer and one was almost within touching distance of Jamie. Fern was too frightened to concentrate, or perhaps the only thoughts that she could send to Timbar were those of alarm and panic. The Firewurm rose still higher in the night air. Rima, acting on his own initiative, swept his tail at Pinch and sent the little man sprawling backwards on to its broad tip, where he lay motionless as he was lifted on to Rima's back. Venior attempted to do the same, but because only one of Jamie's feet was on his tail, the sudden movement caught Jamie off balance and sent him sprawling on his knees by the campfire. Jamie didn't even cry out. He simply knelt on all fours, for he could now hear what Fern and Mrs Mercer could not: the strange and sweet sounds that had entranced Pinch.

Mrs Mercer beat Timbar's back with her fists in vain as the three Firewurms climbed into the night sky. Away over the hill they flew, travelling with awesome speed.

"You cowards, you rotten, stinking cowards!" Fern sobbed. "I'll never speak to you again. You've left Jamie with the Murderings! You've left my brother to die. You're worse than Malvolia, worse than anything." The dragons, distressed by Fern's thoughts of anger and sudden hatred, none of which they could understand, blew a trident of yellow flame before them as they sped away.

Jamie, surrounded by the Murglings, now close enough to touch him, felt as if he was dying. The song the Murglings sang had now become unbearable. He felt as if he was being torn apart. One half of him heard all the beauty in their song, and the other heard all the misery, all the loneliness, all the ache. He laughed and he cried as he knelt, filled with fierce joy and, at the same time, wracked by an awful despair. He was dimly aware that the dragons had gone and that his mother and Fern and Pinch had been carried away; but he couldn't care about it. The fact that he had been abandoned seemed so unimportant and so meaningless compared to the sounds he heard. Suddenly the song ceased.

In the light of the campfire Jamie raised his eyes from the ground and stared at the figures that ringed him, and the fear that he began to feel, remembering that he was on his own, dissolved like smoke. These were not the terrible and dreadful creatures that Pinch had supposed them to be.

The Murglings were tall, tall as young trees, but now that they had come out of the shadows, now that he could see them, Jamie realised that they were not awful at all. Their faces were fair, strange masks of age and youth, neither the one nor the other. They were dressed in robes, the sort of robes that Jamie imagined the Skoddermen might wear with great, voluminous hoods. But, as they threw back those hoods, the Murglings' white hair fell shining to their shoulders like fountains of clear water.

One of the Murglings knelt and stretched a pale hand to touch Jamie's cheek, wiping away the tears that glistened there. Another stooped and lifted him to his feet, gently, as if he was a delicate and rare crystal that might shatter if roughly handled. Two more removed their cloaks and wrapped him against the chill night air, drawing him to the dwindling warmth of the campfire, where he stood, clutching the garments about him.

Suddenly, in one movement, all the Murglings fell to their knees and placed their foreheads on the ground, bowing to Jamie, like supplicants in the presence of a god. Jamie stared into the night sky where a distant fork of three flames flared briefly. Then his eyes fell back to the figures that bent before him.

"Who are you?" he asked, unafraid but curious. "I'm Jamie Mercer from Stubbs Terrace. Why are you all on your knees? What is it you want?"

The nearest Murgling stood. He was at least three feet taller than Jamie, a giant nearly, but he held out his hands to him like a child asking to be pardoned for some wrong. And the hurt in his eyes, when Jamie was unable to respond to his pleading, was dreadful.

"Have you come for the Heart?" Jamie asked. "Is that it? I haven't got it, you know. Mack has that and I truly don't know where he is. I know he means to do evil with it and I'd help you if I could but . . . I can't."

The tall Murgling shook his head. Clearly what Jamie was saying meant nothing to him. He offered his hands again and fell down upon one knee, so that his face was level with Jamie's. His eyes begged. Begged for what? Jamie thought. What could he think Jamie had that might be so important, so vital? The other

Murglings raised themselves and stared at their leader, waiting.

The tall Murgling pointed to the sky.

"The dragons?" Jamie asked. "They've gone, with Mum and Fern and Pinch. You know, Pinch, Keeper of the Copse and the something around here. You frightened them away. You should have said something when Pinch asked you to. You should have come forward and let us know you didn't mean to hurt us."

The tall Murgling tilted his head, confused. He pointed again at the sky, that was filled with stars, and then he pointed at Jamie and nodded. Twice he repeated the gesture; the stars, then Jamie, the stars, then Jamie. And then he nodded, hopeful, thrusting forward his hands again. The other Murglings copied him and, for the first time, they spoke.

"Essillar," they whispered as one, and the sound was like a soft wind sighing through trees. "Essillar, Essillar, Essillar."

"Essillar," the tall Murgling repeated in a louder voice, pointing for the fourth time at the night sky and then at Jamie. Jamie stared up into the black heavens, pricked with the patterns of stars that he could not recognise. He remembered Fern at the window at Ditching, talking to Timbar, and he remembered something that Pinch had said. What was it? "We have no kings and queens, though there was the Starchild, long ago."

"Oh no, no," Jamie said, understanding and waving his hands. "Stars and me? You couldn't be more wrong. I'm Jamie Mercer." He patted his chest. "Me . . . Jamie Mercer. I'm not – I'm not your Starchild."

"Starchild," the tall Murgling repeated, with a little difficulty as if the word was hard for him to pronounce. He touched his own breast. "Mion," he said, and then touched Jamie's hand gently, whispering, "Starchild. Essillar."

Jamie flopped to the ground, swathed in the Murgling robes, and began to laugh.

Mion smiled and then frowned, confused by Jamie's amusement, both pleased and upset by his reaction.

"Oh no," Jamie said. "If only Stephen Burnes, if only Miss Potter could see me now. Me, a Starchild. I don't even know what that's supposed to mean." He grasped Mion's hand and squeezed it.

"There!" he said. "Do I feel like a Starchild? Do I look like a Starchild? Do I?"

Mion withdrew his hand, grinning and obviously pleased that Jamie had touched him.

"Jamie Mercer," he said.

"Yes, that's right, Jamie Mercer, from Stubbs Terrace. A ropey old three up and three down in a ropey old town in ropey old England."

Mion bowed his head, and for a moment Jamie thought that he understood and was disappointed, but when he lifted his head his eyes were filled with joy.

"Jamie Mercer. Essillar!" he cried aloud, throwing up his arms to the stars above.

His cry raised a great shout from the other Murglings and they all rose and came to Jamie, lifting him up with cool hands that felt like petals against his skin. Borne aloft, Jamie surrendered to their touch, and lay back against the soft, strong arms that carried him.

He stared up into the dark sky with all its stars winking down. The Murglings refused to understand. They thought that he was the Starchild, heaven knew why, but they did. Jamie sighed as the Murglings passed the Leestone and carried him off into the dark and gentle Mithacan midnight. He heard them chant in time to the beat of their own steps.

"Mercer! Essillar! Starchild. Essillar! Mercer! Essillar!"

For the first time in his life, Jamie felt important. He felt more than important, he felt needed, special. He glanced at the white hair and the joyful, happy faces of the Murglings, as they marched down the Hill at Ember and into the pitch black of the Mithacan countryside. It could do no harm to play along, he thought.

Fern, his mother, Pinch and the Firewurms were the last things on his mind as the company of Murglings strode surely and purposefully through the darkness. He was Jamie Mercer deep down inside, but on the outside he would be Essillar, the Starchild of the gentle Murglings.

The soft night wrapped them in its dark sheets and Jamie frowned.

"Essillar?" he thought. Where had he heard that word before?

15

Mion

Fern had cried herself into a fitful sleep. Mrs Mercer clung to her and forced herself not to think of what might have happened to Jamie. She could understand the dragons' flight from the Leestone, for hadn't Pinch told them it took a lot to provoke a dragon to anger? They had clearly felt that the safety of three was more important than the safety of one, and had reacted accordingly. She could understand it, but she could not forgive the dragons as they sailed into the night.

She even pressed a hand to Timbar's broad head and tried to send her thoughts into his mind, to calm him and make him turn back and at least look for Jamie, but she hadn't Fern's ability to communicate with these dragons, and Timbar flew on relentlessly, his head and his heart still filled with Fern's confusion and anger.

Venior kept his distance from the others as if in disgrace for not having lifted Jamie properly. Feeling Pinch rouse himself from his trance-like state and struggle to a sitting position, Rima lowered his tail and balanced his jerky flight.

Pinch screwed his eyes up in the darkness and when he spoke his voice was thick and heavy, as if he was waking from an anaesthetic.

"Where's Jamie Mercer?" he called drunkenly, above

the wind of the dragonflight. "Where's the kidling?"

Mrs Mercer was unable to answer for a moment, feeling again the constriction in her throat that threatened to make her cry. She swallowed hard and spoke very quietly. "Back there. With the Murglings."

"Oh," said Pinch, with a frown, not fully understanding.

"Is that all you can say? Oh?" cried Mrs Mercer. "My Jamie's back there and God knows what's happening to him. You, *you* called the Murglings to the Leestone. It was *your* doing. I think the least you could do is make the dragons turn round!"

Pinch hit the side of his head with the flat of one small hand, trying to knock the echoes of the Murglings' song from his brain. "Can't," he admitted. "Can't talk to 'em without the Dragonstone. Can't be done, Looey Smurser. Maybe the podling . . . "

"Stop it! Stop it!" Mrs Mercer shouted, clutching Fern to her. "Stop calling me that ridiculous name, you stupid little man! My children aren't podlings or kidlings or any other pathetic name you use. They're children! Children, do you hear? They can't fight for themselves. They're helpless in this God-forsaken world that they never asked to come to. Why can't you talk and act like a normal human being instead of like some obnoxious goblin out of a cartoon?" She grasped Timbar's tendrils in anger and the dragon roared fire across the sky.

The terrible storm of her words was unbearable and Pinch fell silent. Mrs Mercer suddenly wanted to apologise but she was too choked. It wasn't Pinch's fault that things had gone the way they had. It was she and Mack who were responsible for the danger that now threatened Pinch's world and way of life. She knew that, but she still shook with fury and anxiety.

The dragons sped south, pale beasts with the moon on their wings and the stars in their eyes. They flew for a long time before Mrs Mercer felt Timbar tilt slightly beneath her, a sure sign that he was losing height and preparing to land. She had no idea where they were or how far away they were from Ember and Jamie.

Down, down Timbar flew, sure of the way in the blackness, with Venior and Rima close on his tail. As he swooped lower, he banked and turned along a line of dark shadow rising sheer against the sky. He gave a sudden short call, like the cry of a gigantic peacock, and his call was answered by a similar cry. He turned suddenly, calling again and being answered, calling and being answered, crying aloud for guidance, and being guided in by the beacon of sound that rang through the otherwise silent air. With a long drawn out shriek, Timbar turned so suddenly that Mrs Mercer was almost thrown off balance, and he headed straight for the cliff. Just when she thought that they would crash against the rocks, the darkness engulfed them as Timbar passed into a long cavern, picked and carved out of the cliff-face by countless generations of dragons. They swept by the black shadow of the Guardian, the lone dragon at the cavern's mouth who had guided them in, and along a tunnel so wide that the three dragons could have flown side by side if they had wished, with their wing-tips barely brushing the walls.

The air grew warmer the deeper into the cliff they penetrated and there was a faint light far ahead like the glow of sunrise, only redder and duller. The light increased swiftly and stained the walls, which were scored and pitted. Mrs Mercer glanced across at Pinch. She could see him clearly now in the strange light. He was staring ahead with a fixed expression on his face, refusing to look in her direction.

Then the end of the tunnel flashed by them and the three dragons soared into a cave as lofty and as hushed as a cathedral. They swooped among tall columns of natural stone that sprang from floor to roof, columns so thick that three grown men would only just ring them with their outstretched arms.

Along the walls of the cavern ran broad shelves where a host of other dragons of all sizes roosted, and it was to one of the widest of these ledges that Timbar carried Mrs Mercer and the sleeping Fern. He settled lightly and raised his tail. Mrs Mercer gathered Fern in her arms and was lowered to the rocky ledge.

She reached out a hand and touched the wall at her back, withdrawing it quickly at the feel of the heat there, though the stone ground of the shelf on which she stood was quite cool. As she settled Fern down as comfortably as she could, Venior landed and Pinch dismounted.

"Where are we?" said Mrs Mercer, nervous under the watchful eye of the other dragons there.

"This is Wurmhall," said Pinch, jerking a thumb at the base of the cavern, far below them, where a lake of red water (the source of the cavern's light) bubbled and flared like liquid fire.

"And that's Wurmpool. S'where they drink." He paused. "You not mad any more Looey Smurser?"

"No, Pinch," she said. "I had no right to be angry in the first place. I was – I still *am* – worried for Jamie." And she added, her voice breaking, "What do you think the Murglings will do?"

Pinch's old face creased in deep thought. "Their song . . . " he began. "Their song wasn't doomly, and

I'm sorry if that sounds perthetic, but it's the only way I know to tell it, 'cause whatever you think, I hain't a huming bean. Oh, it was sad and dreary and whatnot, but it was happy and peaceful as well. You sure you heard nothing?"

"Nothing," said Mrs Mercer. "Do you think they were just curious then because you'd sent out a summons from the Leestone? Oh, but if they were, then what did Timbar mean when he told Fern that the Murglings had come for Jamie?"

"Don't know," said Pinch. "And there's no asking him till the podl— till Fern wakes up."

Pinch laid a hand on the dragon's flank. Timbar's eyes were fixed on the depths of the pool far below.

"Attimbarradon, old fellow," Pinch murmured. "You did the best you could." He turned to Mrs Mercer. "And he brought us to the safest place he knows. There's precious few ever been within these walls. Though where we go from here I just don't know."

Far away to the north as the dragon flies, Jamie was, at that very moment, being cushioned in a makeshift bower of soft leaves and branches. The Murglings had garlanded his head and shoulders with night-stock and pale vines with tiny flowers that winked like stars through the dark green foliage. Two of the Murglings had poured a liquid from flasks that they carried and as it splashed into wooden bowls it glimmered with a light of its own. They set the bowls around Jamie like many moons, until the bower was bright as day. Two Murglings brought him fruit and one offered him a dish of sweet water which Jamie sipped at and then downed in one long, thirsty draught. And then they sat at his feet and stared at him with eyes full of admiration and praise.

"Where's Mion?" Jamie asked, studying the Murgling faces which all looked the same to him: beautiful but empty of any strong emotion. "Mion. Where is he?" He felt as if he was a-sail upon a sea of white hair and strange adoring looks.

At the sound of his name Mion stepped into the bower. His face was serious as he said, dutifully, "Essillar?"

"But I'm not . . . " Jamie started to say and then he sighed. There was no point in wasting any effort in trying to shake the Murglings of their belief that he was anything other than their Essillar, the Starchild. It would be far easier to take advantage of their mistake.

"Mion, I have to get back to Mum and Fern and Pinch. There're important things to be done. I have to get to Heart's Hill somehow. There's Malvolia, you see. She's this witch, and she snatched Karrax, and she wants to get to Heart's Hill so that she can steal the Heart which she thinks is there, and all so that she can make you her slaves."

Mion nodded and poured out another dish of sweet water and held it out.

"No, no I don't want another drink," Jamie said, waving his hands for Mion to take it away. "Listen, Mion, I have to get back to Mum. You saw her. She was the lady on the hill-top, the one that rode off on the dragon with the little girl. Mum, like . . . " Jamie pointed to the nearest Murgling woman to him. "Like this lady here. Mum, mother."

Mion lifted a small diadem of white metal from the woman's brow and placed it on Jamie's head.

"Mother," he said, smiling. "Essillar-mum."

"Oh Lord," Jamie said exasperated. "I wish you could speak good old English like Pinch."

Mion nodded. "It shall be as you wish, Starchild," he said, perfectly and clearly.

"Well, why couldn't you have done that before?" Jamie cried. "It would have been so much simpler."

"You did not wish me to," Mion said. "Have I displeased you, Starchild?"

"What? No, you haven't displeased me," Jamie said. "But, please, I'm not your Starchild. I'm Jamie Mercer."

Mion frowned. He lifted a chain from his neck and unclipped the pendant that hung from it. It showed a young boy, with his hands raised, encircling a tiny heart. In the space above the boy's hands a bird-like figure flew.

"You think that's me?" Jamie asked, scrutinising the pendant. "It's nothing like me, really. It can't be me, because I've never been here before. That is, my ancestors are from Mithaca but that was years and years ago."

Mion replaced the pendant. "We have waited years and years," said Mion.

Jamie tried again. "The boy on the medallion looks like me I admit. I suppose that flying thing could be a Chilldrake too *and* the boy's holding a heart, but that's just a coincidence. And speaking of the Heart— "

Mion held up his hand. "Forgive me, but do you wish the others to understand this too, Starchild?"

"Well of course I do," Jamie said. "This affects everybody in Mithaca."

"So be it," said Mion. "We listen and understand."

As quickly and clearly as he could Jamie told the Murglings all that had happened. They listened all right, but where Jamie expected them to at least show some emotion to his story, even if it was only downright disbelief, they merely nodded politely.

"Well?" Jamie said when he had finished. "Now do you see why I have to get back to the others? We have to get everyone together so we can stop Malvolia." Then he added, reluctantly and quietly, " . . . and Mack if need be."

Mion blinked seriously. "We listen and we understand, but we do not understand," he said rather confusingly. "Do you wish that we be alarmed?"

"Alarmed?" Jamie floundered. It was like talking to a machine that spoke back with intelligible but unintelligent questions. "I wish you would understand how serious it is," he said.

Mion bowed his head. "It is as you wish," he replied, pausing for a moment. "The matter is serious for the Mithacans because you think they would not wish to be the slaves of Malvolia the witch. Equally, the Mack that was your friend and who proved treacherous has the same designs on this world, designs with which he will use the Heart of Mithaca to bring to fruition. This also would not be to the liking of the Mithacans."

"That's right," said Jamie, thankful that he seemed to be getting somewhere at last.

"Your concern for the Mithacans is worthy of the Starchild. Your heart is as vast as the Heart itself," said Mion. "Do you wish us to be concerned also, Starchild?"

"Why can't you just be yourselves, and stop talking about the 'Mithacans' as if they were foreigners?" Jamie said, almost shouting with frustration.

"Ourselves?" Mion said. "What else might we be but ourselves? Forgive us, we cannot fulfil that wish, Starchild. Some things are beyond even the power that is yours to command." And there was such a look of hurt and disappointment in Mion's eyes that at first

Jamie didn't appreciate what Mion was saying.

"Power?" he said. Then he realised. Mion and the Murglings had only started to speak English when he had wished it. They hadn't properly understood matters until he wished them to. And now, because he had wished them be themselves, which they already were, they thought that they had disobeyed him. It seemed that the Murglings could be or do whatever he wished.

A glorious idea suddenly sprang into Jamie's mind. "Mion," he said, "how many of you are there?" and he knew instinctively what Mion's reply was going to be. He almost mouthed the words along with him.

"How many of us do you wish there to be?" Mion asked, innocently.

"Dozens," Jamie said slowly. "No, wait . . . hundreds." And he held his breath. Mion bowed, happy to comply with Jamie's wish.

"So are we hundreds, Starchild."

Jamie closed his eyes and breathed a great sigh. He couldn't even begin to understand it, but that didn't really matter in the circumstances, did it? If the Murglings wanted a Starchild then he would be it.

And besides, Mithaca now had an army.

16

Wurmpool

Pinch rubbed his rumbling stomach. It felt like days since he had eaten. His large eyes roamed the stone shelf where Timbar roosted, looking for anything that he might eat. A bit of moss, brown and shrivelled, was the only other sign of life there apart from the dragons, but it was hardly good enough fare for the Keeper of the Copse and Boscage Abouts. Timbar seemed to be sleeping, at least his eyes were shut fast, and his breath was shallow. Pinch stared around at the other shelves that ranged the walls and he started to count the beasts to pass the time. After seventy he gave up and crawled to the ledge and peeped down.

He touched Mrs Mercer's arm and she followed his gaze into the dizzy lower cavern and watched a dragon drink. It lapped at the fire-red waters like a great cat and was not at all troubled by the apparently intense heat. Its dark tongue flashed in and out, drawing the liquid into its beak, then it threw back its head and uttered one long shriek, like a cry of thanks. It spread its wings and regained its perch high along the wall.

"Is it water or what?" Mrs Mercer asked. "Is that all they live on?"

"S'what *these* lovelies live on," said Pinch. "Fire-water, you might say. Don't suppose you thought to bring any of that ham from Ditching with you? Thought not."

Pinch rummaged in the folds of his tunic and brought out a small, flat tin dish. Moisture had collected in small puddles along the stone floor and he scooped up a little to taste it. It was brackish, but drinkable and he wet his dry lips with it and offered some to Mrs Mercer. She sipped and made a face, but dipped the corner of a handkerchief in it to dampen and cool Fern's forehead.

Fern woke, and stared about her for some moments. "Where's Jamie?" she asked.

"We think— ' Mrs Mercer said, trying to sound cheerful. "We're sure he's safe. Pinch is convinced that the Murglings mean no harm. The dragons simply misunderstood our own fear, that's all. We were waiting for you to wake so that you could ask Timbar to take us back and make sure that Jamie's all right."

Fern shook her head. "I'll never speak to them again," she said. "They're all cowards. They could have stayed and fought the Murglings, but they just flew off."

Pinch smiled and sat down by her. "They's not swimping scaredies," he said. "They don't never fight, 'cause they know that if they ever let loose their fire there'd be nothing that could stand up against it."

"I don't believe you," Fern said. "You're making excuses for them." She suddenly pressed her hands to her ears. "Stop it, Timbar," she cried. "I don't want to listen. I won't listen!"

Timbar's eyes were open and he was staring at Fern with an intense look.

"Don't speak to me. Just get out of my head!" said Fern. "You ran away and left Jamie. And I don't believe you when you say it's for the best. That's what people tell you when they can't think of a good reason for anything. They just say it's for the best and shrug their shoulders, as if that makes it all right. Jamie's probably dead, and it's all your fault. So shut up! Shut up and stop talking in my head."

Timbar's eyes flashed and he shot forth his neck. His great beak opened and closed, nipping a fold of Fern's clothing at her back. Despite Mrs Mercer's efforts to stop him he lifted Fern and leaped from the shelf, dropping through the air like a stone, only spreading his wings at the last moment to hover inches from the surface of Wurmpool.

"Timbar!" Mrs Mercer screamed. "Timbar, please. She's only a child. She didn't mean anything. Timbar!"

For what seemed an eternity Mrs Mercer watched Timbar hang above the surface of Wurmpool, dangling Fern from his beak, like a bird of prey with some small catch. She saw Fern struggle briefly and then stay motionless.

"Timbar!" Pinch shouted, alarmed himself now, his voice echoing around the cavern walls. "Attimbarradon N'Werrym!"

"Don't worry," Fern called back, waving her arms to show that Timbar had no intention of harming her. "It's all right. He's not going to hurt me. He only wants to show me something. It's not hot at all here, not hot at all. It's quite cool in fact."

Fern fell quiet, silenced by the sight of the waters below which had begun to swirl slowly, like bath water as it goes down the plug-hole. Only this water didn't disappear. Its red surface smoked.

In her head Timbar's thoughts rang out cold and clear as he told her to look. Fern rubbed her eyes as the troubled surface of Wurmpool cleared. At first she saw only herself, her own face reflected in the dark waters. Then gradually, like a blurred picture swimming into focus, she saw Jamie.

His head was crowned with stars and there were tall figures around him, young men and women with white hair and smiling faces. Jamie was smiling too, amid the throng, laughing and looking happier than Fern could ever remember.

"Is this happening now?" she asked Timbar. "Is that Jamie now, right at this moment?"

Timbar told her that it was.

"Wurmpool shows what is as well as what may be," were the thoughts that Fern heard, and she was so relieved to know that Jamie was safe that she didn't quite follow what Timbar was saying.

"Jamie's safe, Mum!" she called out. "This pool's like a television and you can see what's happening anywhere." And then she thought, "And what might happen anywhere." "Timbar?" she whispered. "Timbar, will the Wurmpool show me what *will* happen? I mean will it show me how everything is going to turn out?" And Timbar's thoughts whispered in her head that it would but that there would often be too many turnings.

"Too many?" Fern thought. "What do you mean, too many?" She felt Timbar's wings beat to rise.

"Wait, Timbar!" she said. "I'm sorry I shouted and said I hated you. Please will you make the pool show me what's going to happen to us all?"

Timbar's quiet thoughts asked why.

"I'd just like to know that everything will turn out the way it should," Fern said. "That's not a lot to ask, is it?"

Timbar's thoughts spoke in Fern's mind: *"The Firewurms do not use the pool's sight for this. It shows* all *that might happen. Many paths have many endings.*

It can be too much truth, too many choices. Too much pain if that which is hoped for comes not to pass. Too much pain if that which is seen there comes to pass."

Fern shook her head. What Timbar was saying meant little to her. All that mattered was that here was an opportunity to find out how this business would end. She pleaded silently with Timbar, while Mrs Mercer and Pinch looked on, unaware of what Fern was attempting. Timbar's breathing became laboured and he shook his head from side to side, straining against Fern's relentless urging. But it was as if he had no choice. Though he could have spread his wings and taken Fern back to the shelf, he did not. Against his will be breathed through his nostrils upon the surface of Wurmpool and told Fern to look again.

The first thing that Fern saw was Jamie. He was smiling, still surrounded by those figures with the white hair, but there was a look in his eyes and a curl to his lip that made her uneasy. On Jamie's head there was a crown, tall and white, and in his hand there was a staff of white wood which he used to beat one of the white-haired figures into a kneeling position at his feet. She saw Jamie scream words which she could not hear but which cowered the crowds before him into submission. Fern shut her eyes. Surely not. Surely that was not the future. Jamie appeared as if he was a prince, a vicious and terrifying lord, cruel and hard and cold and no better than Malvolia. Fern was ready to be taken back to the ledge when the pool cleared.

Now she could see Malvolia, transformed from the dumpy figure that she was in Stubbs Terrace into her giant form. Tall as a tower she stood in the midst of a ring of stones. Her eyes blazed and she held in her now great hand the pebble-like Heart of Mithaca. Her gnarled fingers closed about the Heart and crushed it to powder. All around her fires sprang up and sped away from the stones like a web of flames, spreading and burning everything in their path. Behind Malvolia, in the glowering night sky, all the stars went out, one by one.

Fern was confused, but didn't have time to voice her confusion because the image of Malvolia scattered into a thousand ripples that swept from the centre of Wurmpool and lapped at its edge. As the ripples settled, the image of a face formed. It was an old face that had once been kind and friendly, Fern felt sure, but which now burned with hate and triumph. Fern shuddered. The dark glasses were gone but there was no doubt, it was Mack. His eyes were clear and blue and they stared at her like pools of ice, and the only emotion in them seemed to be one of loathing. Mack too held the Heart of Mithaca in his hand, and white fire leapt from it like lightning that streaked across the surface of the pool and shattered the vision. Then the waters seethed, settling slowly into the last image of all.

It was a street in a red-brick town, a street full of small houses and all of them boarded up and empty. From the grey sky that frowned down on the street, rain fell, dull and heavy as lead. It was Stubbs Terrace and it was empty of all traffic save for three lonely and dejected figures, drenched and weary, who stumbled down the glistening pavement. The rain lashed down and the image of Stubbs Terrace faded into the deep red of Wurmpool.

"Is that it?" Fern thought, and Timbar rose slowly and regained the ledge where Pinch and Mrs Mercer waited.

"Four different futures; four different ways in which things might turn out," Pinch mused, when Fern told them what she had seen. "Can't say any of 'em sound all that swishling somehow. Either we get Jamie all frosty and starkling lordy, or Malvalvolag the Burner, or McFeggerspilth with his eyes back and as bad as the others."

"There's the last vision," said Mrs Mercer, trying to sound hopeful.

"We were home but we didn't look very happy," said Fern. "I'm hungry. Are we going to stay here for ever?"

"Did Timbar say that one of those ways was definitely the way things would turn out?" Pinch asked thoughtfully, trying not to think of food.

"Does it matter?" said Mrs Mercer seriously. "I mean, is it going to stop us trying to rid Mithaca of Malvolia? Or do you just want to give up and let her and Mack settle it between themselves?"

"Neither," said Pinch decisively. He stared up at the cavern roof. "I wonder what time it is?"

"It must be morning," said Mrs Mercer. She felt easier now that she knew Jamie had come to no harm.

"I wonder if Edwyn and Licia have managed to get help?" Fern asked. "I could eat a horse!"

"There's only one way to find out," said Pinch, who at that moment would quite cheerfully have eaten anything cooked. Fern, understanding Pinch's meaning, pressed her hand to Timbar's side and sent the thought.

"Please may we go, Timbar?"

Timbar hesitated, shifting uneasily on the stone ledge as if leaving the safety and the warmth of Wurmhall was the last thing he wanted to do, but he lowered his broad tail and only tossed his horned head as Fern and Mrs

Mercer clambered on to his back. Rima shuffled closer and allowed Pinch to mount. The dragons tested their wings.

"Will the other dragons join us?" said Mrs Mercer. "Surely an army of them would be unstoppable."

There was a strained silence during which Pinch's stomach rumbled and groaned. "Venior says that he will watch in Wurmpool," Fern said, listening to the dragon's thoughts. "If he sees we're in trouble he'll try and make the other dragons come to help. He says . . ." Fern cocked her head as she tried to concentrate. "He says it might be difficult, though. The other dragons are much younger than him and Timbar and Rima. They say they only want Wurmhall and Wurmpool and their own thoughts. They only want to think about the Starchild that made them, and not fight against creatures who are weaker than they are and who don't know any better. Does any of that make sense?"

"Yes," Mrs Mercer said. "In a way, it does." Pinch was rubbing his chin as if something had just jogged a memory.

"Starchild again," said Fern. "I wish I knew what that was, Pinch."

"Eh, what, Fernling?" said Pinch. "Oh, aye, aye. All in good time."

The air lurched as the dragons took to the wing. Timbar and Rima plummeted from their ledge and stopped to drink at the pool before they rose and swept in and out of the tall columns that supported Wurmhall. All the other dragons remained on their perches, silent and wary, as Timbar and Rima flitted like moths in and out of the shadows that the red light of Wurmpool cast.

Timbar banked and left the cavern, hurtling into

the chill of the long tunnel and the cold air of the Mithacan morning. The sun was rising, chasing away the night with a pale half-hearted glow.

"Jamie!" Fern thought as the shock of clean and open air slapped her face. She pressed her cooling palms against Timbar's head and sent her own private thoughts into Timbar's mind. "Find Jamie, quickly, Timbar."

And Timbar gathered speed with each agitated thrust and thwack of his wings. He also had seen the visions that the pool had shown Fern.

They must find Jamie, before the first of the visions came true.

17

Broken Heart

Mack lay on his back with his face turned to the stars. The night air was cool by the small stream to the north of Ditching, but he seemed not to notice the chill. He grasped the Heart in his right hand, and stared at the stars. They were clear and cold and they looked back at him with frosty stares of their own, as if they knew what it was he had done. His dark glasses lay at his side, where they had fallen from his face as he had crashed to his knees, far from the place where he had left the children and Mrs Mercer paddling.

He had taken an enormous chance, stumbling blindly, clutching the stolen bag. He had moved quietly at first, so as not to alert the others to the fact that he was missing. Then, sure that they would not hear him, he had thrashed and staggered through the undergrowth, using the stick that Jamie had begged from Pinch, to beat away the small obstacles in his path and to warn him of the larger ones so that he could avoid them.

When his absence was discovered he was far enough away not to hear their frantic cries for him to come back. But his flight away from his friends had also taken him in a sweeping arc so that he was back on the bank of the same stretch of water that he had left, only half a mile or so downstream. There he had fallen, tired and breathless, and there his dark glasses had dropped from his face.

Scrabbling in the bag and scattering its contents, he had found the box. With shaking hands he'd fumbled in vain for the moves to open it. Desperation made him impatient and he'd cursed aloud until he'd heard the click that released the lid. Feverishly he had tipped the stone into his hand and it was at that very second, still with his eyelids closed, that he had seen the sunbeams dance on the water like fireflies.

Dazzled and puzzled by a light that he thought he would never see again, he had turned his face to the heavens and seen the flash of blue and white that was the sky and the clouds. He'd lowered his face and looked to the right and left, glimpsing the green of the grass and the trees about him.

Mack could see again. It was only borrowed sight and hazy, like looking at the world through frosted glass, but he could make out enough detail for it not to matter. He'd placed a hand over his eyes. It made no difference; his hand might as well not have been there at all. The Heart was acting like the eyes he did not have. He could see. Still with one hand over his face he slipped the Heart into his jacket pocket. Instantly the familiar darkness returned. Then he lay on his back and, not caring if he was being pursued, not caring if he was discovered, he pulled out the Heart again, and had gazed at the sky.

The blue turned to rose and the rose to the indigo of night, as Mack lay with only his own thoughts for company.

"I didn't intend this," he whispered to the dark and glittering night. "Not at first. Please believe that. I could have taken the Heart from Louise in Stubbs

Terrace, but I didn't. I was strong enough then to resist the temptation; strong enough then not to give in. But . . . " He fell silent, seeing the stars even more clearly than the soft moon, though they were far more distant. "But I knew the legends," Mack reasoned. "And I have some passive magic still. I knew from the first second that my fingers touched Louise Mercer's brow, that not only had she Mithacan blood but that she was a descendant of the Starchild and that Jamie, her only son, was the true heir to the power of the Heart. I knew that, once in Mithaca, his very presence would rouse the Murglings. Yes . . . " he decided, struck by the sudden thought. "Yes, that was it. I was worried that, if they found and claimed the Heart, they would simply return it to the Henge, where Malvolia would come and claim it and all would be lost. I knew . . . "

He knew he was lying. He could invent any number of good reasons for why he had taken the Heart from Mrs Mercer, from the one person, from the *only* person to whom Karrax could have entrusted it: to be held by her, in safe-keeping, until its rightful heir should be born.

"But Jamie would not have known how to use it," Mack argued with the stars, as if it was they who had planted the last thoughts in his mind. "He's young. He couldn't possibly know how much power there is in the Heart. Power to make and power to destroy. It would have been like giving a loaded gun to a child and leaving him alone to play.

"I took the Heart so that he would not misuse it and harm either himself or others. He would have tried to use its power to stop Malvolia and would have only succeeded in harming himself, or worse, he might have failed to use it and then Malvolia would have claimed it and . . . "

And it was another lie, another excuse to justify the theft and his own greed and desires.

"So what if I took the Heart to claim its powers for myself!" His voice fell to a whisper. "It was not out of greed, not this time. I took the Heart to save Mithaca, to stop Malvolia. I am the only one strong enough and, yes, wise enough to do it. When the witch is destroyed I will renounce those same powers, make whole the stone and surrender it to the Starchild. I will teach him then how to use its powers properly and sensibly. I will . . . I will."

One star amongst all the rest seemed to burn more fiercely in a silent final challenge for Mack to tell the truth.

"I will be the Lord of Mithaca," Mack said quietly, honest for the first time. "I would begin in earnest to put right the wrongs that I have done, and then I would go on, obsessed with my own mightiness and majesty until I committed wrong again. Never, never would I surrender the Heart to another . . . "

Mack suddenly began to laugh. "And I see no reason to now. Who will make me? Malvolia? What are she and her Skoddermen to me? The Queen Bee and all her drones can buzz and busy themselves about the countryside in a quest that is doomed to fail before it starts! Ha! Or do you think the Mithacans will overthrow me this time? No, they had time before, time to gather a force that they cannot hope to assemble now. Why, I only have to take the Heart . . . " Mack raised his fist " . . . and say the words. I know them, you know, I know the words to set free the power of the stone. The Mercers don't. They could never hope to know, even if they are the heirs to the stone; even though they are the kindred of the Starchild!"

Mack staggered to his feet.

"Ach inshoras!" he cried aloud. "Ach inshoras bei tahonn, bei talithon y aldha andhrovadh! Tuar meidar, tuar diskhelion, tuar d'neglin Mittakar! Ish behan . . . "

The stars in the night sky flared. "The last word," they seemed to cry. "Say the last word, Caspar McGee, and more power than you can have ever imagined will be yours to command."

Mack tottered at the brink of that power, his lips moving but making no sound. His whole body trembled. He tried to stop his ears against all the voices that were ringing in his head.

"There was once a magician, a very great magician . . . Blind fool . . . As much power as a flat battery . . . My eyes were opened the moment they were taken away . . . Oh, Mack, you were once a baddie . . . "

All those voices: Mrs Mercer's, Malvolia's, his own, Fern's, all mingled in his brain; and then a small, clear voice rang out like a bell through the torrent of half-remembered snatches of conversation, calling him back from the edge of the pit in his soul into which he almost plunged.

"The past must teach the present, Caspar McGee, so that the present may prepare for the future. The future is the Starchild's to inherit."

Mack lowered his head. "No," he said, sinking to one knee. He lifted his face to the stars and his cheeks were wet with the tears of his struggle. "No. Then, perhaps I might have sealed the spell. Now, no . . . never."

Mack wiped his cheeks and took a deep breath. For a long time he knelt under the starlit sky, listening to the sound of the stream and the distant cries of night-creatures. Then he rose and, using the Heart for his eyes, and by the light of the moon, Mack made his way through the midnight countryside.

Caspar McGee had made his choice. Somewhere out there was the true and rightful heir to the Heart of Mithaca, and Mack was going to find him.

18

To Battle

Jamie stood at the top of a low rise with Mion at his side and surveyed the massed army of Murglings that covered the hillsides and beyond. Actually they looked more like a peaceful congregation than an army but then, Jamie argued, it's the number that counts. He felt light-headed, like the time he had sneaked a glass of sherry from the cupboard at Stubbs Terrace and had drunk it like lemonade, just to see what the taste was like. He had been sick afterwards, and the carefree light-headedness had subsided into a roaring headache and a churning stomach. He hadn't ever wanted to taste sherry or anything like it ever again.

Now, he felt a similar intense and giddy joy. Seeing the Murglings standing before him, all ready to do whatever he asked of them, he felt powerful. He felt as if there was nothing that he couldn't do if he put his mind to it and his heart into it. He, Jamie Mercer, the Starchild of the Murglings, was going to save Mithaca.

"How did you do it, Mion?" he asked. "How did you make yourselves to be so many?"

"It is as you wished," said Mion simply, as if there was no need for any explanation other than it had been the wish of the Starchild that had swelled their numbers.

"Well, I don't understand it. But I am glad," said Jamie smiling.

"The Starchild is pleased?" Mion asked.

"The Starchild is very pleased," said Jamie. "Now, do you know where Heart's Hill is?" Before Mion could answer, he added, "I wish you to know where Heart's Hill is. And I wish to go there as quickly as possible. Mum and Fern and Pinch will be safe enough with the dragons."

"So be it, Starchild," Mion took Jamie's hand and started to walk away with him.

"I want the others to come too!" Jamie said. This was going to be harder than he had first thought. He would have to remember to say exactly what it was he wanted since Mion and the Murglings took everything so literally. "It's they who are going to do all the fighting, you know."

Mion stopped and beckoned to the others to follow. Like a white tide the Murglings started to move. They crossed the countryside, keeping the Leestone to the north and the sun, which stood at ten in the sky, more or less in front of them for the first few miles, so that they headed east. Jamie found the going hard. Walking through open country wasn't like taking a stroll down a pleasant lane. There were no roads, not even tracks, and this part of Mithaca seemed to be all up hill and down, with meadows of tall grass, small woods and coppices, thick natural hedges and rills and ditches.

Once he stumbled and Mion, full of concern, offered to carry him. After a moment's hesitation Jamie agreed and was hoisted on to Mion's shoulders, from where he had a fine view. Then they marched, a white company, heading for Heart's Hill.

In a flat meadow of tall grass Jamie decided that

they should rest a while. They had walked for hours and, while Mion didn't seem to tire at all, Jamie's back ached and his eyes stung with tiredness. Mion set him down and stood quietly by while Jamie flopped on to the grass.

"Starchild?" Mion asked.

"Mmm?" Jamie mumbled, finding it hard to stay awake and lying back into the soft swathes of green. A cool wind fanned his face and relentless waves of sleep washed over him.

"Starchild, what is fighting?"

"Fighting?" Jamie pondered. "Fighting is punching and kicking and biting if you have to."

"I see," said Mion thoughtfully. "And you wish us to do this to each other?"

"I certainly don't!" Jamie said, amused by the idea of the Murglings brawling amongst themselves. "I want you to do it to Malvolia and the Skoddermen."

"I see," said Mion again. Jamie knew that he didn't at all and he waited for the next question.

"Why?" Mion asked. "Why must we fight Malvolia and the Skoddermen?"

Jamie sat up. "Because, if you don't fight them and if you don't show them who's boss, then Malvolia will take over Mithaca. I told you all this before. I wish you would listen."

"I listen, Starchild," said Mion. "Kicking and punching and biting the Skoddermen and Malvolia will drive them away and this will please the Starchild."

"That's right," said Jamie. Then a sudden thought struck him. "I expect you'll have to kill quite a lot of them though, before they admit defeat. Yes, quite a lot I should think."

"Kill?" Mion repeated gently. Jamie sighed. Mion's

stupidity was really starting to get on his nerves.

"Kill," he said. "Punch them until they die. Hit them with sticks and stones. Strangle them until they stop breathing. Kill!"

Mion seemed to be struggling with this concept. "Might we not ask them to leave? If their leaving is what would most please the Starchild then what matters which way it is done?"

"Because they wouldn't do it, you idiot!" Jamie said. "Look – you'll just have to trust me. I know what's best. You do what I say, and stop asking questions and arguing. I *am* the Starchild!"

Mion bowed his head. "Then it shall be as the Starchild wishes, as it has been and as it always will be."

Jamie was angry with Mion for even daring to question his orders. Here he was doing everything he could to save a world that was only a part of him because some old and forgotten ancestor once lived there, and all Mion could do was argue.

"Course," Jamie said, a little thrill of malice in his voice, "I expect some of you will get killed too, I mean, I can't see the Skoddermen just standing there and taking it all and besides, some of them have knives that they're bound to use, but it won't matter. I shall just wish for more of you and keep on doing that until the Skoddermen all give up or die. And when Malvolia sees what she's up against, *then* she'll think twice about crossing me."

Jamie smiled and stared at the white clouds that drifted lazily across the sky. It was a wonderful plan and, like all wonderful plans, it was so simple. Jamie saw Mion still frowning, and he felt charitable enough to let the Murgling speak.

"Go on," Jamie said. "One last question."

"Starchild?" said Mion after a long silence, during which Jamie felt more and more pleased with himself.

"Yes?" he said, trying in vain to sound patient.

"What is 'die'? You said that you wish us to kill the Skoddermen so that they die. You said that some of us would also be killed and die. What does it mean?"

Jamie propped himself on one elbow. "I can't believe you're so stupid!" he said, but he could tell by the look in Mion's eyes that he really did not know. "Dying is like killing, except it happens to you. To die is . . . is to stop breathing. Your heart gives in and your brain stops thinking and you, well, you just die." A sudden thought struck him. "Oh, but listen, you mustn't let any of the Skoddermen come near me. Do you understand that? You mustn't let anyone harm the Starchild. You mustn't let the Starchild be killed or die. Promise?"

"No one will harm the Starchild," Mion said softly and sadly. "It shall be as you wish."

"You'll all go to heaven, I expect," Jamie said. "And don't ask me what *that* is because I really can't be bothered to explain. Just think of it as a place where all good people go when they die, and what you're going to do is a good thing, because it'll save Mithaca and that's what the Starchild wants, do you see?"

Mion said nothing, made no movement. He simply gazed out over the Murglings, all of whose eyes were on Jamie; all of whom were there to serve the Starchild and do his bidding. Jamie wondered for a moment what was going through Mion's mind, and then he decided that he didn't much care anyway.

"I think it's time we were getting on. Pick me up and carry me," said Jamie.

They continued for a short way up the side of a

sparsely wooded hill. For all his size, Mion moved as swiftly and as silently as the sea of Murglings at his back. As he reached the top of the hill and passed through a small copse Jamie caught sight of the valley below them. His heart gave a jump and he banged Mion on the shoulder to stop.

"Look!" he hissed through his teeth. "It's her. Malvolia. Get down, Mion. Get down before she sees us."

It certainly was Malvolia. Dressed in her pink coat and seated on a crude wooden throne, she was being borne along the bottom of the valley. A host of dark-clothed figures trailed in her wake. Karrax would be in the midst of them, Jamie thought.

As he watched, Malvolia ordered her bearers to stop. The Skoddermen lowered her chair and Malvolia stood up, stretching her legs. She looked so small and insignificant from this distance that Jamie felt strong and sure, and he pictured himself stretching forth a hand and rubbing the witch out like a small and annoying fly.

Aloud to Mion he whispered, "This is it, Mion, you know. This is our chance to take her by surprise. We're hundreds and she's only got her dumb Skoddermen. And I bet only a few of them have knives and things. The Murglings can swamp her and I'll rescue Karrax. It's brilliant!"

Mion's eyes were dark and troubled. "Is this where we die?" he asked.

"No, no," Jamie said quickly, fearful lest Mion should refuse to send the Murglings into battle. "I want you all to forget everything I said about killing and dying. Just tell them to get sticks and stones and go down there. Quickly, before she decides to be off again. And hurry back!"

"So be it, Starchild," said Mion.

Jamie stayed under cover on the brow of the hill, biting his knuckles with excitement. Silently, like a white tide, the Murglings surged over the brow of the hill and down into the valley. The swarm of Murglings coursed down the slope as Malvolia looked up from where she stood. For a second, just for one second, she looked as if she was going to panic at the numbers that rolled towards her and her Skoddermen. The whole hillside was covered with white-haired Murglings that swept like an avalanche. Jamie was thrilled. It was going to be over so quickly. Then the Murglings stopped in front of the Skoddermen, turned round and looked to where Jamie lay, and it was only then that he noticed how they had armed themselves. Some carried small sticks no bigger than twigs, pulled from shrubs or found on the ground, while others held small stones and pebbles.

"What . . . ?" Jamie stammered. "What are they doing? What use are twigs and pebbles? And why have they stopped? Mion? Mion!"

Mion came silently and lay beside Jamie. "It is as you wished, Starchild."

"What do you mean, it's as I wished?" Jamie cried, tearing his eyes away from Mion and staring down into the valley. Malvolia had reseated herself, waiting.

"Why don't they kill the Skoddermen?" Jamie said.

"What is kill?" Mion asked, and for one moment Jamie thought that he was playing some sick game. And then his own words came back to him. "Forget what I said about killing and dying."

"But – I didn't mean— " Jamie began and then was stunned into silence by a terrible cry from the valley below as the Skoddermen, at a signal from Malvolia, rose as one and bore down upon the Murglings. Here and there, a sudden flash of sunlight on steel revealed drawn Skodder-knives and, as the gentle Murglings all gazed to their Starchild, the Skoddermen cut into them like a scythe through a swathe of grass.

Murgling men and women fell to the ground, stabbed or cudgelled, trampled or thrown down, and they didn't even use their arms to defend themselves, let alone fight back. Malvolia herself, hardly able to believe that the Murgling army was not retaliating, abandoned her disguise and rose ten, twelve, fifteen feet in her anger, until she towered above the horrible one-sided battle, like a giant scarecrow-wife. She raised her arms and white fire lashed from her fingers, sizzling through the ranks of the immobile Murglings, blasting them and burning them and casting them down. Again and again she threw out her awful fire.

Above the cries of the Skoddermen, and the crackle of Malvolia's blasts, Murgling voices were raised in a heart rending cry. It was only the one word, called in desperation, hurt and confusion, but it cut through Jamie with an edge keener than the sharpest Skodder-blade, and with a power fiercer than the worst of Malvolia's blinding fire.

"Essillar?"

Sickeningly the massacre continued until there was not one Murgling left standing on the valley slope. Throughout all those long minutes Jamie, numbed by the Murglings' cry for help, help that he was too stunned to give, shut his eyes and wished that the slaughter was not happening in the valley below him.

"Make her stop!" Jamie said at length. "Please, Mion, make her stop it."

"Starchild," said Mion, not taking his eyes away from the dreadful destruction of the Murglings, "I have no command over the witch Malvolia. I cannot order the Skoddermen to stop what they do."

"Then," said Jamie, his face pressed into his hands. "Then make more Murglings. No don't. Yes do! Make more Murglings and this time, tell them to kill, *make* them kill. Make more Murglings. I am the Starchild! I don't want this to happen. I want it to be different. It – it isn't my fault, you know. I didn't want to be the Starchild. You made me. *You* made me say I would be the Starchild. Make more Murglings, now!"

Mion stared beyond Jamie, to the valley below. "From what do I make more, Starchild?" he asked.

A smell of burning reached Jamie's nostrils; a smell of burned cloth, burned grass – and something else that he refused to think about.

But he made himself look.

The hillside was still white, like a long meadow after a fall of snow, but here and there the Skoddermen, themselves like dirty footprints, marred the whiteness and made it unclean. Black tracks of spent fire and spots of dark red, like dragons' eyes, stared back at Jamie. Malvolia had chained her fire and had shrunk back into the small shape of Miss Dummel, and she was made all the more hideous by her unthreatening, earthly quality. Dark smoke drifted and melted in the afternoon sun. The Skoddermen cheered their miraculous and absurdly simple victory, sheathed their knives and gathered about Malvolia like flies around a sore.

Malvolia scanned the hillside for any second wave of attack but she knew that there would be none and, almost as if she was refreshed by the killings, she set off with renewed energy on her journey to Heart's Hill.

And into the stillness of the desolation came the slight sound of a Starchild weeping, and the soft wind of the sigh of the last of the Murglings, together and alone . . .

19

Prisoners

"Starchild?"

Mion touched Jamie's shoulder lightly as he lay on the grass. "Starchild?"

Jamie woke up with a start and stared at the blue heavens. For a moment he lay and gathered his thoughts and then sat bolt upright. He was still in the meadow where he had first decided to rest and Mion was bending over him wiping away his tears.

"You wept in your sleep," said Mion. "What disturbs you so?"

Jamie stared past him to where the Murglings were still assembled in their patient ranks on the hillside. The wind billowed their spotless gowns, and their eyes were turned to their beloved Starchild.

"Oh, Mion," Jamie said, his voice shaking with the terrible relief that accompanies the waking from a nightmare. He gripped Mion's sleeve to convince himself that he was not still asleep.

"I was dreaming," he said. "It didn't happen, none of it did. It was only a dream."

"A terrible dream to make you weep so," Mion observed.

"It was," Jamie said, nodding his head frantically. "It *was* a bad dream. It was the worst dream I've ever had. It was horrible. *I* was horrible. I thought that one fight, one battle and it would all be over. And it was, in a way, though not the way I hoped." He stared into Mion's blue eyes. "Killing's not the answer," Jamie said. "Nor fighting. At least, not my way." He ran a hand through his hair, the memory of the terrible cry of the slaughtered Murglings in the nightmare still ringing in his ears.

"I hope you mean that," said a voice at his back. "I sincerely hope you mean that, for your sake."

Jamie twisted round on the ground and his eyes met those of Malvolia.

"She came while you slept," Mion explained. "She said that she knows you and that I should waken you. I was glad to do it for you seemed so troubled." Mion frowned. "This is not the one you call mother-mum, is it?"

"It certainly is not!" said Jamie, scrambling to his feet.

Malvolia smiled. "Well now," she said, in the same sort of voice one might use when meeting a friend on a country stroll. "Well, fancy meeting again like this."

Mion might be fooled by her attempt at good manners, thought Jamie, but he wasn't.

"Where's Karrax?" he demanded.

"The Chilldrake?" Malvolia said. "Oh, quite safe, for the moment. He did struggle so though, when we arrived here. I'm afraid I had to calm him down a little. Couldn't have him skipping off and hurting himself, could I?"

"This is Malvolia, you know," Jamie told Mion. "Or should that be Queen Du Mal?"

Malvolia gave a light laugh, girlish and simpering. "Can I help it if Fate has decided that it be so?" she asked and clicked her fingers. From the bushes at her back five armed Skoddermen stepped forth, brown-robed and hooded. "Besides," Malvolia added, the tone of her voice changing to one of contempt. "What's in a name anyway, *Starchild*? A brat by any other name is still a brat. Who's the half-wit with the lap-dog eyes?"

Jamie blushed, not for himself but for Mion who stood behind, wary, with his hands on Jamie's shoulders.

"Mind your own business," Jamie said, tossing his head.

"Everything here *is* my business," Malvolia said, a trace of menace creeping into her voice. "I have just made it so. Tell me – the dear Skoddertrash are a little unclear on this point – who *are* your friends?" Malvolia waved a hand to all the Murglings. "It's quite a little army, isn't it?"

Jamie couldn't be sure, but he thought he detected a trace of envy in Malvolia's voice – or was it alarm?

"I think you'd better give in, Malvolia," Jamie said, surprising himself with his defiance. "Tell your – things – to throw down their knives and bring Karrax before I . . ."

Malvolia raised an eyebrow and gave a lop-sided grin. "Before you what?" she said, feigning a frightened stance.

"Just do it," Jamie said, reaching up and placing his hand on Mion's. Malvolia wavered, casting a wry glance at the assembled Murglings. Jamie didn't know how many more Skoddermen there might be lurking hidden, but he guessed that Malvolia was weighing up the numbers of Skoddermen she had against the Murgling army.

"I think . . . not," said Malvolia at length, and she folded her arms.

"Right," said Jamie. "Right then!" and he started

to tremble so much that Mion held him tightly. Jamie opened his lips to speak, to tell Mion to order the Murglings to attack, but the words would not come, not when the memory of his dream was still so clear in his mind and his heart. Jamie's defiant stare faltered and the witch laughed. Malvolia had called Jamie's bluff and the look of superiority in her eyes made Jamie want to run and throttle her where she stood.

It was not even stalemate, for though Malvolia might still have been a little dubious of the Murgling numbers, she knew now that they would not be used against her, though she could not guess the real reason why. She still had her own formidable powers too, as well as a Chilldrake as hostage.

"Can I see Karrax?" Jamie asked, trying not to sound beaten.

Malvolia's eyes narrowed. "Oh yes," she said darkly. "You can certainly see the Chilldrake, because you're coming with me. In one way or another you have caused me a great deal of trouble, and I don't like having to change my plans. I had no intention of coming to this world so soon – though my dear Skoddertrash are some compensation – and I certainly had no idea that you would follow and dare to threaten me with a rag-bag rabble of simpletons. No, I can't afford to leave you running loose around Mithaca. I shall have to keep my eye on you, at least until I can spare the time and the energy to deal with you more permanently."

"You could kill me now," Jamie said rashly, knowing that it was what Malvolia intended to do, sooner or later.

"Yes . . . " Malvolia agreed, as if debating the point in her own mind. "Yes, I could. But there are questions that I want answered. How, for instance, did you manage to come here when *I* have the Chilldrake? I despise having to rely on the whims of some mindless lizard should I ever want to travel between worlds. You obviously accomplished it; such knowledge would prove very useful to me." Malvolia paused and stared at Mion. "Perhaps the blond vegetable brought you here? No matter . . . you will tell me in time. There is also the question of who else might have come with you." Here Jamie started, much to Malvolia's amusement. "Ah, I gather, then, that you did not come alone. And despite myself I find I admire the way you manage to inspire such apparent devotion from so many; albeit they are simpletons, I am nevertheless intrigued."

"He is the Starchild. We do as the Starchild wills. The Starchild must not be harmed," said Mion, and Jamie wished he hadn't.

"Quite, Bimbo . . . " said Malvolia, her eyes still on Jamie. "But now we really mustn't spend any more time in idle chatter, must we? You, Starbrat, will order your sheep to stay here and not follow. I am sure they will amuse themselves until I have decided their place in my new kingdom. They could watch the grass grow, if that's not too much of a mental strain. The tall half-wit goes with us too. I should hate for you to be parted from such a devoted and witless pet. We can't have him pining away for his master. Get your things together. We are leaving."

Malvolia disappeared, leaving some Skoddermen to watch Jamie and Mion. The Skoddermen's thin fingers twitched at the hilts of their long knives.

"Tell the others to wait here please, Mion," Jamie said quietly. "Tell them we'll try not to be away too long. And tell them – tell them not to worry. Everything will be all right."

"It is already done, Starchild," said Mion.

"Oh, and one other thing," said Jamie. "I don't want you to call me Starchild any more. Just Jamie will do. It – it's what I'm used to."

"So be it, Jamie," Mion replied. "And now we follow the witch Malvolia?"

"We don't have much choice," said Jamie.

Malvolia and the rest of her Skoddermen were waiting in the valley. Jamie and Mion walked silently and quickly, the ranks of Skoddermen parting before them until they came to the centre of the throng. There the cage containing Karrax rested. From her raised throne, Malvolia cackled as she noticed the despair on Jamie's face when he saw how sick the Chilldrake was.

The Chilldrake's skin, which before had shimmered, was now dull and flaking. His eyes were half closed and their deep blue was dimmed and filmed over. He didn't even raise his head when Jamie stretched a hand through the bars and stroked his hot, shivering back.

"What have you done to him?" Jamie demanded.

"It's a slow poison," said Malvolia, with malicious glee. "Ultimately lethal, though as long as he gets a few daily drops of an antidote, he should last a while longer. The antidote, by the way, is in the possession of one of the Skoddermen, just in case you were thinking of trying to steal it from me. Do you know, I forget which one of them has it. They all look the same, don't they? But I expect you have the same trouble with your lot."

"I hate you," Jamie said, through clenched teeth, doing his best not to let Malvolia see he was upset.

"I expect you do," said Malvolia. "But you will obey me, if you want to last longer than the Chilldrake."

"If you promise you'll make him well again when

we get to Heart's Hill," Jamie said, "Mion and I will do what you say."

Malvolia tutted and shook her head. "Not only does he try and extract promises from me, but he seems to know my plans as well," she said as if she was talking to herself. "I suppose it was Mouth McGee who told you about Heart's Hill. Don't bother to try and deny it. I can see it was by your eyes. It couldn't have been anyone else. The idiot by your side hardly seems to know what day it is."

"Malvolia seems not to like me, Jamie," said Mion.

"Ha! Jamie is it now?" Malvolia sneered. "Soon changed his tune. He learns fast. I neither like nor dislike you," she said to Mion. "You are insignificant and I shall keep you alive only as long as it suits me to; so watch your step. Which goes for you too, ex-Starchild. And *that* is the only promise you'll get from me. We have wasted enough time already. The sooner I get to Heart's Hill the sooner I can— " Malvolia stopped, her eyes wide with alarm. "McGee . . . " she hissed. "He came with you, didn't he? Answer me, you little swine!"

Jamie stared in sullen silence. Should he admit that Mack was in Mithaca too? Or would the knowledge only throw the witch into a panic, with no telling what she might do? He smiled to himself inwardly, thinking what Malvolia would say and how she would react if she knew that Mack at this moment had the Heart.

"I know what you want," Jamie said. "But you won't get it, you know. You'll be stopped just like Mack was the first time. And they'll probably put out your eyes too. They'll— '

Malvolia lashed out with her foot and kicked Jamie a fierce blow in the face. He staggered back and Mion sprang forward, his face, probably for the first time in his gentle life, dark with anger.

"Mion, no," Jamie said quickly, seeing Malvolia raise a hand in the gesture of fire-blasting that he had seen in his dream.

"Please, Mion. I'm not hurt."

Jamie tasted blood in his mouth where his lip had banged against his teeth. Malvolia was breathing heavily.

"Any more attempted heroics from Tall and Witless and he dies," Malvolia snarled. "And any more unwanted comments from you and you suffer the same fate. Now get moving."

Malvolia exercised her unnatural and unspoken control over the Skoddermen and they all started to shuffle forwards at once, pushing Jamie and Mion along, leaving the valley and striking eastwards to Heart's Hill. It was now early afternoon and the sun was still high in the sky, hot and unclouded.

Jamie and Mion walked as close to Karrax's cage as the Skoddermen would allow, and Jamie tried a little detective work. He reasoned that the most likely of the Skoddermen to possess the antidote would be one of the four who carried the cage, one at each corner. He fell a little way behind the cage and kept his eyes on the four carriers to see if any of them tried to slip something to the sick Chilldrake. Sure enough, after a little while, the left rear Skodderman pulled out a small vial of blue glass and forced a drop or two down the weak Chilldrake's throat.

At least that was something, Jamie thought. At least he now knew where the antidote was. He picked up a small chalky pebble from the ground and managed to squeeze close enough to the Skodderman to be able to mark his robe with a small white cross. The other

Skoddermen seemed not to notice what he was doing, or if they did, they seemed not to care. Jamie wondered if their docility was natural or the result of some spell of Malvolia's. Either way he remembered how the fingers of the Skoddermen had twitched about their long knives and he shuddered. He was thankful that he could see nothing of their faces under their dark hoods. It wouldn't do to underestimate either the Skoddermen or Malvolia.

What Jamie didn't know was that Malvolia had posted one lone Skodderman at the front of their company to scout the way ahead and to make sure the way was clear of any challenge. It was this leading Skodderman who had spotted the massed Murglings. There was also a single Skodderman a little way behind the company to check for stragglers and report on anything that might be following them.

This last of Malvolia's followers was now out of sight of the main company. To make doubly sure that none of the Murglings tried to follow, he was standing in the small wood above the hill where the Murglings patiently awaited the return of their Starchild. Satisfied at length that they would do as they had been ordered he turned to follow the rest of the Skoddermen.

He never made it out of the wood. After only two steps, a black shape stepped swiftly and silently out of the shrubs, grasped the Skodderman from behind and caught his neck in a grip so fierce and unshakable that the Skodderman's neck snapped before he could draw his long knife. The unseen assassin rolled the crumpled Skodderman over and removed his dark robe, slipping it over his own head, before dragging the body into the bushes. Then, as quickly and silently as he had killed, this new Skodderman set off and followed the others . . .

20

Mithaca Rises

The two dragons rushed out of Wurmpool and into the light of day. They beat their wings and rose higher and higher, finding rising currents of warm air that lifted them with little effort. Using their great wings like gliders, they swept in vast circles over the Mithacan countryside with Pinch, Mrs Mercer and Fern gripping tight and gasping for breath. At that height the clean, cool air made everything very clear, and the distant pale, purple mountains seemed but stepping stones to an even stranger world, swathed in mists beyond.

Before, they had flown over a world that seemed empty of any life, save for the glorious green of Mithaca's landscape. Now, even at this height, Fern could see that the whole of Mithaca was moving. Either Pinch's message from the Leestone had finally reached enough ears, or the Borderers, Edwyn and Licia, had been truer to their word than anyone could have guessed, because almost as far as they could see the landscape teemed with life.

Figures, small as ants, moved through the countryside, gathering into groups here and there as they travelled, or moving singly. They all hastened with one purpose and one direction. Fern shielded her eyes from the sun and marked the spot in the far distance to which all that hurrying life seemed to be heading. She saw a tall hill with one blue-black stone rising from it like a finger pointing to the heavens. It was Ember and the Leestone where Pinch had first raised the alarm and where the Mithacans were gathering, answering the call.

"What now?" Mrs Mercer shouted to Pinch and the little man waved an arm in the direction of Ember, like a general waving on an army. Mrs Mercer understood. Jamie was safe; the thing to do now was to rally the Mithacans, explain why they had been called and enlist their help in ridding their world of the disease that, one way or another, she and the children had unwittingly brought to Mithaca.

She spoke to Fern, who placed her hand on Timbar's powerful head and said, "Go to Ember, to the Leestone, Timbar. We have to talk to the people there. We have to make them understand why they've been sent for."

The big dragon obeyed immediately, thumping his wings and heading for Ember, with Rima close behind.

Fern gazed upon the land below and tried to fix in her mind where everything was. Ember she could see, drawing nearer all the time, and it was strange to think that it was the same pitch-dark place where Jamie had been left with the Murglings. Ember was only a low hill, but the way it rose out of the surrounding shrubs and trees, with the tall stone at its summit, gave it an air of isolated mystery.

Somewhere beyond the Leestone, to the north, was Ditching, nestled in its small orchard where they had first seen the dragons. Beyond the pale silver flashes of the stream that she glimpsed through the woods and trees, was the spot where they had all arrived. Fern sighed; it seemed such a long time ago. She cast her eyes over the landscape and wondered where Jamie was.

She wondered too whether he was still the same, or if he had already turned into the fearsome vision she had seen in the Wurmpool. She shivered and tried not to think of that as Timbar banked, circled and swooped, spiralling down to Ember.

There was a group of Mithacans already there when they arrived, talking and gesturing amongst themselves, but they all scattered on seeing the dragons land. Pinch dismounted from Rima and went to stand by the Leestone. There was a look of grim determination on his face that more than made up for his lack of size. He stood in the shadow of the beetling stone and shouted, "To me, Folkings and Peoples! I called you all, Pinch, Keeper of the Copse and Boscage Abouts. Come on, come on. The dragons are our friends and allies in this war."

Slowly, a few crept out of the bushes, their eyes wary and their hands gripping the few weapons they carried. There was one old man, not unlike Pinch himself in size and appearance, who skirted around the dragons and came to stand in Timbar's shadow.

"War?" he asked, his voice gritty and dry with age. "What war? We know nothing about a war. Some waspy-tongued Borderess came by our village last night, shouting and bawling that everyone who could had best get to the Leestone and quick if they knew what was good for them. She also said that she would be here to explain why. What is the matter? Where is she?"

"That would be Licia," said Fern. "She's probably still rounding up the others. But we can explain, can't we, Pinch?"

"Aye," Pinch agreed. "All in good time, when there are more here. Can't go telling it all in drips and drobs, though. I should have no voice left. Sit down, good father, and be patient a while longer, until there are more of us."

"I know you," said the old man. "You're old Nip's lad. What are you doing mucking about with Fire-beasts? And how is your old dad?"

Pinch screwed up his eyes, scrutinising the old man. Then he brightened. "Why, Master Gollin Carver; it is you, isn't it? I thought you sounded familiar." Pinch's voice dropped to a subdued mutter. "Thank you for asking, Master Carver, but my old dad passed away these four winters gone, rest his bones and boots." He spotted a small sack dangling at the old man's belt. "You wouldn't have fetched any grubbage with you, would you? Only we hain't had so much as a crumb in our throats since . . . since . . . "

The old man gave a wheezy laugh. "Just like your old man," he chuckled. "Peckish, are you? Well, there's bread and cheese and a flask of spring water here as you're more than welcome to. But I'm getting on in years and I don't know as I can wait to hear what's happening to make everyone so jittery and flustered, so I'd thank you to tell me, 'twixt mouthfuls as it were, just what in the name of all that's sensible is going on!"

Mrs Mercer and Fern joined Pinch in the makeshift meal, and while they ate, and while Fern stared with ever widening eyes at the crowd that was gathering, Pinch explained as quickly and as clearly as he could. Throughout the tale, Master Carver wheezed and tutted and laughed or shook his head where the story warranted it, and finally slapped his side when Pinch had finished.

"Then you were right to raise the alarm, and well done!" he said, a fierce twinkle in his eye. "It's just like the old times again, when we all rose against McGee.

We put a stop to his tricks then and bless me if we won't do the same for Du Mal. Fancy thinking we're such easy meat to be carved and sliced. And McGee back again, is he? Didn't have enough last time? Heh, we'll see about that."

Many had assembled by now on the hillside at Ember. And some had gathered in a small circle about Pinch and his friends, trying to catch wind of why they had been summoned. For Fern, at least, the sight of so many strange and different beings was magical. At last here were her trolls, tall and grey like old stones walking; here were slight, willowy folk with long golden hair (Fern thought these might be elves) with serious, sad faces and wondering looks. There were creatures with skin like trees, silvery-grey like birch-bark in the women and mossy-brown and gnarled like sycamores in the men. There were horned folk and folk with fur; blue-skinned and straggly haired cavemen types who wore nothing more than a string of beads about their necks. And there were what Fern would have called the ordinary folk, men and women pretty much like Edwyn and Licia and of all ages, and these mingled with a multitude of others, all chattering, muttering and asking each other the questions which they expected Pinch (since he seemed to be doing most of the talking) to answer.

Seeing so many, and with his belly at least halfway full of Master Gollin Carver's grubbage, Pinch stood up and called for silence. Then he gave a speech that even Pinch didn't think was in him. It was a rousing, roistering, daredevil, up-and-at-'em-to-death-and-glory sort of speech. But at the same time it was calm and deadly serious. He reminded the Mithacans of their freedom, a freedom that had almost been taken away twenty years before (and there were some there that remembered and nodded their heads sagely). They were free to go their own ways and live their own lives in peace, and he demanded to know what they were going to do about it now that this freedom was threatened again. He spoke for the benefit of those that had children, children who would be forced to grow up in the shadow of Malvolia's (or Mack's) unnatural and bottomless hunger for power and the desire to rule. Would those mothers and fathers sleep easy in their beds at night, knowing that their offspring would grow up to expect only slavery and fear? They had swimping well better not! He spoke of the countryside, the green and rolling, peaceful land that they all knew and loved, but which they had probably all taken for granted. He confessed he didn't know what Malvolia's plans were, but he knew enough about her to be able to guess that her desire for power and mastery would benefit nothing and nobody except the witch herself and the treacherous Skoddermen.

And he spoke of the magic of Mithaca, the magic that was the very breath and being of all that dwelt there. The magic that Malvolia and Mack meant to get their hands on and twist to their own evil purpose; the magic that made their world and kept it where it was; the magic that made all folk different and yet which kept them all in peace, accepting each other's differences for what they were. How would they feel when the very thing that *was* Mithaca's specialness and glory was taken and turned against them. How would it be if the trolls were beaten and driven out simply because they were tall and grey and different? Because that's what would happen, Pinch cried. Folks would look at other folks and see that they weren't like them and wouldn't accept that they had the *right* to be different!

It was a speech laced with a feeling and a fire that even the dragons understood. Throughout it all, Timbar and Rima remained calm and pensive, their eyes half-lidded and unfocused. And at the end of it Pinch's knees were trembling and his throat dry and parched. A shout rang from the lips of every creature there, a shout of defiance towards Malvolia and the erstwhile wizard McGee, and a cry of support for the little Keeper of the Copse and Boscage Abouts, who had stirred their hearts and kindled their fighting spirit. Fern cheered with them too. She didn't understand half of what Pinch was going on about, but she caught enough of its flavour to guess what he meant. It was a pity, she thought, that Buzz Beddows and the Stargang weren't truly real. They would have known all about what Pinch was saying; it was pretty much the same sort of thing that Buzz always said to the crew of the *Astrogon* just before any battle with Revoltron and his dread hordes.

"A brave and noble speech," said a voice from the throng, and Edwyn stepped forward. He had ridden in unnoticed, and there was a light of admiration in his eyes that made Pinch cough with embarrassment.

"If I could have made such a speech to those I met then there would be twenty times more the numbers that have assembled here." Edwyn's eyes roamed the hill. "Still," he said, "what we may lack in numbers we make up for in spirit, thanks to you, Master Pinch."

"Where's Licia?" said Fern.

"My sister still gathers what aid she can find," said Edwyn. "Though her tongue is sharper than mine and she finds it hard to convince others that their world is being threatened. Yet, she and what fighters she can find, will be at Heart's Hill when the time comes." Edwyn paused. "Though, whether we *all* will is another matter."

"What do you mean?" Fern cried. "Didn't you hear everybody cheer just then? They're not afraid. They'll fight Malvolia and her devils until they drop."

"I did not say that they would not," Edwyn replied. "But you three may ride the dragons at will and be at Heart's Hill on the back of the wind. Licia and I have steeds, and can cover the distance in time."

"Oh," said Fern, understanding. "Yes, I see. You mean how are all these people going to get there? I hadn't thought of that."

Neither had Pinch and he swore under his breath. "We'll just have to get marching and arrive when we can," he said. "There's nothing that Malvomangler can do when she gets to Heart's Hill, 'septing rant and rave when she finds the Heart not there."

"One thing troubles me," said Edwyn. "I have covered many miles last night and this morning, and spoken to many and yet I talked with none who had seen McGee. I saw no sight nor sign of him myself. If it is true as you say, and I do not doubt that it is, that he has the Heart, then why is he so silent and secretive still? To possess the Heart and its secrets of this world was his one desire when last he was here. It seems strange that he has not taken the opportunity to do that now, when he is unopposed and free."

"Maybe he has, already," Mrs Mercer suggested grimly, "and he's just biding his time." To her surprise Edwyn disagreed strongly.

"Nay. We should have felt the Heart break, here where our own hearts beat. He has not used it yet, save maybe to borrow its eyes where he has none."

Fern remembered what Pinch had said about the stone "sniffing" out the way for Mack.

"Like Radar or something, you mean?" she said. "Or like the scanners on the *Astrogon*?"

"Strange words," said Edwyn, frowning. "I know not what they mean." Fern was about to try and elaborate when Mrs Mercer suddenly cried out and held her head.

"Mum?" said Fern. "What is it, what's wrong?"

Mrs Mercer screwed up her eyes as if she was in great pain. "A ringing noise . . . " she stammered. "Oh! It's like, like lots of voices, all talking at once, only I can't hear what they're saying."

Fern looked at Pinch and Edwyn, who shook their heads, hearing nothing. Mrs Mercer was obviously in distress but they were unable to help her. She clutched her head and seemed to find it difficult to talk.

"Wait . . . " she cried aloud, as if to someone not there. "Wait, and not so loud, not all at the same time. Oh!"

It was Pinch who saw them first. Five small shapes that flitted through the air, southwards towards Ember, in a bobbing, frantic flight that was accompanied by what appeared to be a cloud of white smoke. On they came, dark and unrecognisable at first, like little bats in a snowstorm, and then closer until Fern could see the sunlight glinting off their white bodies and the blue of their eyes. And as the flying things drew nearer the pain and the ringing in Mrs Mercer's head grew worse until she almost screamed for it to stop. When it did, she could have cried with relief, as five identical Chilldrakes flapped and karked and krooed above her head.

"Ai Akhildrakori! The Snow-wurms," Edwyn marvelled. "Your mother hears them speak, Fern? This is what troubles her?" He eyed Mrs Mercer with a special reverence and wonder.

Mrs Mercer was breathing deeply. She had finally managed to calm the Chilldrakes, or at least she had managed to shut them out of her mind. She stood in the middle of a small blizzard, while four of the Chilldrakes settled on her arms and shoulders one by one. The fifth, a little unsure, flew to Fern and hovered in front of her face, staring.

"Is it Karrax?" Fern asked, reaching out an arm for the Chilldrake to land on. It ran its beak along her fingers as if sniffing, but it stayed in flight. "How did he escape?"

"It's not Karrax," said Mrs Mercer, closing her eyes to concentrate. She opened her mind tentatively to the little dragons. "It's very hard to tell what they're saying. They all talk at once," she said, trying to think them calm. "There," she said after a moment. "That's better."

The snow disappeared suddenly, and the Chilldrake that was flying in front of Fern landed on her shoulder, digging in with its sharp claws, just as Karrax had done back in Stubbs Terrace.

"Good Lord!" Mrs Mercer exclaimed, lost in mental conversation with one or more of the Chilldrakes. "I can't remember all those long names. Is there nothing shorter?" She touched the Chilldrakes one at a time, saying as she did so: "Pineryl, Ralawn . . . what? . . . oh, yes, Skiffarax and Iscaramar. And the one you have, Fern, is called Gidwen. She, oh . . . " Mrs Mercer looked troubled. "She's Karrax's mate. They've come because they heard the first of Pinch's calls from the Dragonstone at Ditching, and they want to do what they can to help. They're upset because . . . " Mrs Mercer stopped and looked at the others, unable to continue.

Gidwen, perched on Fern's shoulder, gave a soft "kroo-kroo" and hung her head.

"They can feel it inside them," Mrs Mercer said. "They say they've felt it for a while now, faint at first and then getting stronger all the time. A feeling of . . ."

"A feeling of what, Looey Smurser?" Pinch asked.

Mrs Mercer shook her head. She wouldn't say; she couldn't say, not while Fern was there listening. How could she put into words the misery and the heartache that the little Chilldrakes were feeling? How could she tell Fern what the Chilldrakes had just told her – that instinctively they knew Karrax was dying?

Edwyn came over to Mrs Mercer and clasped her hand. "The Keeper of the Copse and Boscage has a rare ally in thee," he said stiffly though sincerely. "It gladdens my heart to think that thou art with us, Essellin-antar." Then he dropped on one knee and placed Mrs Mercer's hand to his forehead. "Had I known before, I would have paid thee due homage."

Fern looked at Pinch and wrinkled her nose. Pinch shrugged, and Mrs Mercer drew her hand away, a little embarrassed to think that all those strangers were watching Edwyn's strange actions.

"You mean you think I'm somehow special because I can understand the Chilldrakes?" Mrs Mercer asked. Edwyn looked up and his eyes registered his disbelief.

"Thou dost not know?" Edwyn asked, rising. "And, if he saw that thou didst not know, did the Keeper not think to tell thee?"

Fern wished that Edwyn would stop speaking like Moses, and say instead exactly what he meant.

"Tell her what?" said Pinch. "I didn't need to tell her

she could talk to Chilldrakes. She knows that already. Besides, t'ain't no great shakes; the podling can talk to the Werrym, too. What you gone all uffish and starchy for, eh?"

Edwyn resumed a normal, though quieter tone of voice. "Chilldrakes and Firewurms, Keeper. Akhildrakori and the Werrym. Does it not stir faint memories of the tales that your mother told you at her knee?"

Pinch thought for a moment, while Mrs Mercer and Fern exchanged looks. Suddenly, Pinch slapped his forehead.

"Strop me with a feggler's spracket!" he cried. "The podling and their umpteen-and-ninety-times-great-grandferdaddy was from this place. Oh, I deserve to be parbroiled in mudge and lubkin's spittage. Of course, Essellin-antar!"

He turned to Mrs Mercer. "Star-kin," he said, as if the one word explained everything. When Mrs Mercer shook her head, none the wiser, Pinch pursed his lips.

"I oughtn't be the one to tell you this, Looey Smurser, and then again p'raps I ought to have told you way back at Wurmpool, when I had the thought on the tip of my toggle, but then I'm an old crogger and sometimes I forgets things as I ought to remember— "

"Pinch," said Mrs Mercer, feeling the Chilldrakes dig into her shoulder, urgently and painfully. "What are you and Edwyn talking about?"

"You can talk to Chilldrakes," said Pinch. "The podling can talk to dragons without using a Dragonstone. There was only ever the one person as could do that, Looey Smurser; him what made the draggers and the wummers in the first place, yonks and yonkers gone. It can only mean one thing, Looey Smurser."

"Which is . . . ?" Mrs Mercer asked.

Pinch bowed his head. "Why, your umpteen-and-ninety-times-great-grandferdaddy must have been the Starchild," he said.

21

Armada of Dragons

Mrs Mercer looked blank; Fern looked extraordinarily pleased to think that she was descended from someone so mysterious-sounding. She had been rather taken with the idea of there once being a Starchild in Mithaca; it had Buzz Beddows' stamp all over it. But to know that she was a descendant of the Starchild was another matter entirely. She beamed at all the Mithacans and felt like waving. Pinch and Edwyn smiled as the whisper ran all around the gathered Mithacans that the kindred of the Starchild were amongst them.

"I think we ought to sit down and talk about this," said Mrs Mercer, quietly.

Pinch and Edwyn nodded as one. "And we will. Great matters need great chattage," said Pinch. "But not now, eh, Looey Smurser and little Starpod. First things first. We have to get to Heart's Henge afore Malvollywog does. We can talk on the way, on the wing."

"Keeper," said Edwyn. "Is there not a problem in what you say?"

Fern thought that Edwyn was going to start rubbishing Pinch's plans again, like he had done before at Ember, but Pinch scratched his head, unoffended.

"And what would that be, Master Edwyn?" he asked.

Pinch now seemed to regard Edwyn as an equal.

"Far be it that I dash cold water on the fires of our haste, but there is still the matter of transport for our army. Dragons have ever been the steeds of the Starchild, and rightly shall his offspring ride them, but, however inspired our feet, I think that they will not make up the distance that the witch has already covered. And, moreover, an army has need of arms if it is to fight."

"You don't have to worry about either of those things," said Fern, pointing to the southern sky. "Look! Venior did it. He got them all to come!"

From the direction of Wurmhall the air was thick with dragons. Large and small, young and old, they had all left their roosting shelves and hurried at Venior's bidding. Venior himself was leading them. Like a dark cloud they hurtled along and filled the sky above Ember, blotting out the sun with their outstretched wings and casting a cool shadow.

"Yahoo!" Pinch cried like a schoolboy, throwing his red hat up into the air, and Mrs Mercer couldn't help but smile at the delight with which Pinch jumped and danced.

"It is truly a day of wonders," Edwyn whispered, a broad smile on his face. "Never have the Werrym been seen abroad in so great a number."

"Not even the last time?" Fern asked as the cloud of dragons circled overhead and started to land.

Edwyn shook his head. "Not even then, though perhaps matters are doubly perilous now and enough of a provocation for the great beasts to act. Besides, the Werrym came ever to the aid of the Starchild. They could do no less for his kin." Edwyn turned his eyes from the sky. "Well, Master Pinch," he asked mischievously. "What say you now? Do we camp here for the night or do we hasten to Heart's Hill and waylay the witch?"

"You will pardon me for saying so," said Pinch, hardly able to contain himself. "But what a gormlish question, Master Edwyn. Of course we go now! You just try and stop us. Are you taking your horse or riding with us?"

"I . . . " Edwyn said, faltering at the thought of riding the dragons. "I am not worthy."

"Rubbish!" said Fern. "Pinch has ridden one, and if he can, then so can you." She stepped on Timbar's lowered tail. "Come on! You can ride with me. It's fun, once you get used to it." Then Fern shouted to the Mithacans: "And all the rest of you! Get on a dragon and hold tight!"

Edwyn hesitated, but only for a second. He took his bow and quiver from his horse's saddle and copied Fern. Together they were raised to Timbar's back, as the other Mithacans gingerly followed suit.

"I like Edwyn," said Fern to Pinch. "He reminds me of Buzz."

"When this business is over," said Pinch, stepping on to Rima's tail, "you must tell me more about this swishling Buzzboy. He sounds like my kind of fellow."

"I will," Fern promised, already on Timbar's back, and then she spotted her mother, standing lost in her own thoughts. "Mum? What's wrong?" she asked.

Mrs Mercer seemed far away. She had begun to feel again the overpowering sadness and hurt of the little Chilldrakes and their concern for Karrax. "Nothing," she said, then she became alarmed when she noticed Fern on Timbar with Edwyn at her back.

"Oh no. You're not going, young lady," she said. "We

are staying put right where we are. If there's going to be fighting I— " She stopped herself suddenly faced with the silent accusation of cowardliness from hundreds of staring eyes, not least those of Pinch and Fern.

"Oh, Mum," Fern said. "How can you say that? It's partly our fault that any of this happened in the first place. You can't back down now. You just can't! You're a Starbit. You just have to see it through."

"Podling," said Pinch from Rima's back, "maybe I was a little hasty. Perhaps you should stay here until it's all over. I – I've gotten quite fondish of your ugly face. It would be a pity never to see it again."

"Which is what'll happen anyway if you go and get yourself killed while me and Mum are stuck here, hiding away while everybody else fights!" said Fern. "I don't care what you and Mum say, I'm just as much a part of this as any of you. I'm going." And she sent a quick thought to Timbar who instantly rose into the air. "You can ride with Pinch!" Fern called to Mrs Mercer.

As if Timbar's taking wing were a signal, the other dragons rose too. Mrs Mercer settled behind Pinch and watched Timbar and the slight, determined figure of Fern sail to the head of the swelling armada. She whispered proudly, "Turnling good grit, that one."

"Couldn't have put it better myself, Looey Smurser," said Pinch. "I 'spect she gets it from her mam."

Like wasps swarming, the dragons headed east. Fern felt Edwyn wobble and steady himself as he tried to get the feel of the unfamiliar steed beneath him. He was holding on to Timbar's natural reins so tightly that Fern was worried he might hurt the dragon.

"Tell me about the Starchild," she said, wanting to know and hoping that talking would take Edwyn's mind off the possibility of falling.

"When all the world was dark," Edwyn began, "and before the lamps of the sun and moon were kindled and hung in the sky, the Starchild fell from the heavens to Mittakar. It was a barren plain then, from north to south, from east to west, little more than a dismal desert, bleak and cold and uninhabitable. The Starchild walked there in the desolation but his mind and heart were filled with thoughts of beauty, thoughts which fell from him like seeds and which buried themselves in the earth. In his right hand he held a golden brooch; in his left hand a silver ring, and on his brow there was a bound circlet set with a gem from his home, a source of great power to build and unbuild. The brooch and the ring he threw into the sky, where they hung, spinning and dancing, and the brooch became the sun which spun the one way, circling the earth; and the ring became the moon, which spun a different way, so that sometimes it is seen in full and sometimes only in part. As the brooch spun, its clasp pricked the fabric of the heavens and let through the lights beyond light."

"The stars!" Fern said, listening intently.

"Aye, the stars," said Edwyn. "From whence he came. The Starchild saw the stars which were his home and, because they were so distant, he began to weep, knowing that he could never go back. His tears became the rains and the rivers and they watered the earth, coaxing the buried seeds of his thought into life. They blossomed into the trees and flowers and the grasses, the sight of which eased the Starchild's sorrow."

A sudden gust of wind buffeted Timbar and Edwyn put one arm around Fern.

"Please go on," she said.

"To ease the loneliness he felt, the Starchild took sun-fire and fashioned the dragons. The dragons lived and breathed, and were his favourites. He bid them fly, to take him as high as they could so that he might glimpse his home and call upon his brothers and sisters to fetch him away. Alas, it was too far for his cries to be heard and the dragons brought him back to Mittakar."

"And what happened then?" said Fern.

"Knowing he could never return home, the Starchild fashioned things that reminded him of it, to lessen the ache he felt. Next to the dragons, he made the Moargelingas, shaping them from moon-fire, and so like his distant brothers and sisters that, ever afterward, they always had a special place in his heart, and he in theirs. They were fair to behold, and gentle. They helped him gather clay to shape all other creatures, those that swim, those that fly, and those that run on four legs or crawl upon the earth. And from that same clay the Starchild also made Men."

"You say that as if it was a bad thing," Fern whispered, feeling the strength of Edwyn's arm.

"Men looked upon the Starchild and were jealous. Jealous of his art, jealous of his special love for the Moargelingas. The Starchild brought forth all sorts of creatures for Man's comfort and company. He took dragonscales and created the Akhildrakori, the little Chilldrakes; and all so that Men would not think they were loved any the less than the Moargelingas."

"Did all this really happen?" asked Fern.

"Edwyn smiled. "So run the tales," he said. "It is said that the Starchild even chose to grow old with Men, to show how much he loved them. Dragons and Moargelingas, though they may be slain, though they may mate and raise offspring, do not wither or fade. As long as there is the sun and the moon, they will endure. The older the Starchild grew, the more he realised that he would never convince Men of his love for them, and the more he desired to find some way he could return home. 'Tis told too that when he grew to adulthood he took himself a wife and that she went with him when he left Mittakar in search of one road that might lead him back to the stars."

"And she was my whatever-times-great-gran?" Fern breathed. Sarah Mellor was going to just shrivel when she heard this.

"It was the Starchild's wish that, if ever any of his kindred returned to Mittakar, they who remained should know them by their talents. The female of his kin would have the ability to converse with one or other of the dragonbreed and enjoy their protection; while every first-born male of direct blood would be rightful heir to the power of the Heart, and have the special protection of the— "

"I know!" cried Fern, bouncing up and down and shooting her arm in the air as if she was answering a question in class. "He'd have the Moargelthingies. But do you know what they are Edwyn? I've worked it out! They're what Pinch calls the Murglings . . . and that's why they came for Jamie. But what *is* the Heart; where does that fit into all this?"

"The Heart was his gift to any of his kindred who might find their way to Mittakar. The stone from the circlet on his brow; the source of the power that made all things save the sun and the moon. That remained in Mittakar, dulled and seemingly lifeless, but there to be claimed when the time was right."

"But . . . " said Fern, frowning. "Aren't there lots of us? I mean, the Starchild would have had children who went away and got married. And their children would have children, wouldn't they? There'd be cousins and aunts and nieces everywhere. Why is it only us who are special?"

"The bloodline of the Starchild's first-born son runs strong in you."

"Ooh," Fern wriggled. "I have to tell Mum. How long will it be till we get to wherever it is we're going?"

"I have never ridden a Werrym before," Edwyn confessed. "I have no way of telling. Heart's Hill rises in Eastfold."

Over wood and field, over stream and lake, the fleet of dragons flew eastwards. Fern was impatient to tell her mother all she knew but it helped to look down and watch the earth slip by or to stare ahead and wonder what sort of a place it was where they were bound.

At one point Fern was puzzled by what appeared to be a field of snow some way down to her left. Then she realised it was a host of people like a crowd at a concert, all dressed in white and silent as if they were waiting for the music to begin. "Hooray for Licia," she thought, never having seen a Murgling in daylight. "I bet that's the army she's got together. I just wish they'd get a move on."

And only a little further on she caught sight of a dark crowd, winding its way along a dry river bottom. At the head of the throng, on her makeshift portable throne, Malvolia raised her head and stared into the sky. Fern immediately told Timbar, and she could feel the fires rumble in his throat.

"Don't do anything hasty," Fern told him. Malvolia might look small and insignificant now but Fern had seen her stretch into that awful figure with the blazing eyes.

"Let's get to Heart's Hill first and wait," she whispered to Timbar. "That'll make her madder than ever to think that we'll be the first at the place where she thinks the Heart is. She'll be fizzing and spitting like a mad cat."

Timbar soared higher into the sky followed by the other dragons.

Some way behind, Mrs Mercer was having trouble with the Chilldrakes. Close now to the cage where Karrax lay, the little dragons could sense more than ever that one of their number had not long left to live. Gidwen, understandably, was the most distressed. Her blue eyes looked as if they would burst into flame at any second. She was making so much snow in her distress that the thick swirl of it made flying difficult for Rima and the other dragons nearby. Mrs Mercer's eyes were shut tight and she was sending desperate, reassuring thoughts to the Chilldrakes, and Gidwen especially. She didn't even notice the Skoddermen below.

The flight of dragons, disturbed a little by the curbed anger of Timbar, began to call, one to the other, their cries rising in volume and pitch until the whole dragonfleet must have been heard halfway across Mithaca. The swarm gathered speed, leaving the dark smear of Skoddermen far behind. The Chilldrakes settled into a brooding silence, ignoring all Mrs Mercer's thought-promises about Karrax's safety. It seemed to her that Gidwen was already in mourning for her mate.

Fern stared ahead with eyes half closed against the wind of Timbar's flight. For hours they travelled until, just as the sun started to fall in the west, Fern at last felt the wind on her face lessen as Timbar slowed. She peered ahead. In the distance, the flat plain rose gently through green meadows and heaved itself into the only hill for miles. Heart's Hill looked like a small mound and it wasn't until minutes later that Fern could appreciate its true size. Man-made or natural, it stood proud of the surrounding countryside, as isolated as a pyramid rising from a desert. Fern could see also that there was something built on the summit.

It was a circle of pairs of standing stones, large and weighty, and on their heads equally heavy stones were laid, so that the whole was a ring of squared archways. And it was to this bare and windswept place that Timbar now headed.

There were few, airborne on the backs of the dragon, who had ever been to Heart's Hill, but there was not one who had not heard of it at some time in their lives, either in tales or songs. Some tales told that Heart's Hill had once been the home of giants, long ago passed away, who had raised the mound and the stone circle as a palace for the moon. Some songs told how the stones there had grown suddenly overnight as a protection for that which they stood guard over, and that if one day their guard was ever challenged, they would uproot themselves and crush whoever dared come there with malice in his heart.

This was Heart's Henge, the ancient guard that circled Heart's Ease; the simple stone casket where the Heart of Mithaca had once lain.

"Heart's Henge!" Pinch yelled to Mrs Mercer, feeling Rima bank and fall. "There we make our stand."

22

Before the Storm

Timbar and Rima chose the sanctuary of the Henge itself for their landing place, while the other dragons and their riders settled about the western slope of Heart's Hill, facing the direction from which Malvolia would arrive.

As soon as all the dragonfleet had landed, Edwyn and Pinch took charge, organising the Mithacans into some sort of defensive formation. Fern ran to her mother and, in a gabble of excitement, retold the legend of the Starchild.

Edwyn appointed a commander from each of the different races who had answered the call to arms, and it was to these he now gave his orders. Mrs Mercer realised how thankful they ought to be that Edwyn had come with them and not ridden on later, for he drew upon his own training as a Borderer and he gave his orders with an authority out of keeping with his youth.

No one was sure what Malvolia would do when her own force reached Heart's Hill, but Edwyn was preparing for the worst. He ordered the large and lumbering trolls, with their thick, impenetrable, stony hides, to form the first line of defence. Knives would not harm them, nor bites and scratches, and their heavy stone axes would do the greatest damage where it was most needed. There was little cover on the slopes of Heart's Hill and the trolls would act as shields for the others who had no weapons other than the stones that they might pluck from the ground.

The blue-skin cavemen formed the next line: many of them had hunting spears which could be thrown from a distance. Edwyn had noticed too that the majority of the blue warriors carried small bone knives. The rest of the Mithacans he organised in tiers about the Hill, according to their strength and numbers. On the upper slopes of Heart's Hill sat the dragons, motionless and unconcerned. They had done their task, they had brought the makeshift army from the Leestone at Ember to Heart's Hill, and now they waited. Edwyn eyed them ruefully.

"Would that we could count upon Werrymfire, Master Pinch. Our ragged army needs weapons and it is said that nothing can withstand the breath of the Werrym when it takes light."

"That's Flemmings for you," said Pinch. "We should be grateful that they gave us a speedling flight. We can't expect any more, though having Looey Smurser and the Starpod here can only be to our advantage. If the Flemmings ever once thought that either of them were in serious danger then, whoosh! Stand back or be toastage."

"Aye," said Edwyn thoughtfully. His keen ears had heard a sound from far off; the sound of hoofs. Pinch heard it too and he scanned the neighbouring landscape for sign of the riders.

"There!" said Edwyn, pointing north-west of the Hill. "Licia, and six – no, seven Borderers. She must have ridden to the Northern Marches for help."

Pinch did a quick sum on his fingers. "Hum, that's a fair distance," he said admiringly. "I shouldn't care to bet which of 'em is the most fashed, Licia or the stalliorse."

"If I know Licia," said Edwyn, "she will be fired with the thought of her first true battle. She beats me often in mock-combat and she will do her utmost to ensure that her fighting skills do us justice if they are put to the test."

They waited as Licia gained and ascended the slopes of Heart's Hill. Edwyn greeted her with pride, kissing her lightly on the cheek, before saluting her and the other riders more formally. Of the seven Borderers with her, four were much older than Edwyn, and yet they all accepted Edwyn's authority. They took their posts below the summit of Heart's Hill, stringing and testing their bows in the shadows of the great stones.

Edwyn and Pinch surveyed the scene.

"I wish there was more," said Pinch. "Do you think . . . ?"

"I think nothing," said Edwyn. "Save that we will do our best when the time comes and that, if we fall, we fall with courageous hearts given freely in a true cause. There is no more to think about, Master Pinch."

"Aye, and what about me, then?" said a dry voice. It was Gollin Carver. From the folds of his baggy clothes he had produced a small sword, no bigger than a bread-knife.

Edwyn laughed and clapped the old man on the shoulder.

"May your sword be not sheathed until it has drunk its fill," he said.

Master Carver bowed stiffly. "And may each of your arrows fly true to their mark," he rasped.

"And now we wait," said Pinch.

Mion held Jamie's hand as they walked in step with the Skoddermen. Malvolia willed the Skoddermen to maintain an extraordinary pace, fired as she was with the thought that tonight she would break the Heart of Mithaca. She realised the extent of that power she was hastening to claim. A mighty power it was, one that could create gardens where there was but desert. It could breathe life into the strangest forms of life where before there had been but the wind and dry, empty spaces. But, above all else, the power of the Heart could unbuild, destroy the very things it had been used to make.

Some small thrill of such power Malvolia felt as she hurried her Skoddermen on, lashing the weak-willed creatures with her mind. She was heading for a moment that she had hungered for all her life but which she only realised was possible when the wizard McGee had come crawling blind, blasted and babbling to her door twenty years ago. Soon she would be All-Powerful, able to do, make, undo and unmake anything and anyone. Soon, *she* would be the centre of Mithaca, its guiding force and its true queen.

Jamie and Mion knew nothing of her black thoughts as they struggled to keep up with the company. Jamie felt lost, abandoned and small; and if it had not been for the warmth and the strength of Mion's hand in his own, he might have given up all hope there and then.

He kept a watchful eye too on the cage where Karrax lay, hardly breathing now, a bundle of grey skin and bones, wasted by the poison that Malvolia had fed him. Jamie had made a silent promise to himself that, whenever and if ever the chance arose, he would get the antidote and save Karrax. If he could do nothing else, at the very least he would try and rescue the Chilldrake. But that meant staying close to the Skoddermen who carried the cage and, in particular, to the one that he had seen with the tiny bottle of antidote.

The Skoddermen seemed agitated too, nervous almost, and from time to time one or other would give a short grunt, as if he had been roused from some deep sleep. Perhaps Malvolia was over-reaching herself. Perhaps controlling all these Skoddermen was more than she could manage. Jamie kept that thought in his mind and quickened his pace to keep by the cage, despite the ache in his legs.

Mion offered to carry him when Jamie stumbled and grazed a knee on the rocky ground.

"No, Mion. No. I'll manage," Jamie said. "It can't be far now."

"As you wish – Jamie," Mion said, lifting him to his feet.

"Don't lose sight of the cage," Jamie whispered. "Don't lose sight of Karrax."

And Mion replied, "I shall not."

Suddenly a shadow fell over them and all eyes gazed upwards. It was smoke, Jamie thought at first, a long trail of smoke in the sky, like the wake of a jet, but it was no aeroplane. Malvolia knew it too and, through her, so did the Skoddermen. They wavered, feeling Malvolia's surprise.

It was the tremendous flight of dragons, dozens and dozens of them, all heading for Heart's Hill. At the head of her company Malvolia shielded her eyes and glared upwards. She considered throwing off her disguise and rearing into the sky to blast the impudent challengers, but the dragons swept higher, out of her reach, and on to Heart's Hill. As they passed, their cry rang out stark and clear.

"Look, Mion," Jamie said, and he was not pointing to the sky but to the Skoddermen, who were faltering and staggering, the dragon's call blocking Malvolia's domineering will from their minds.

"Quick! Where's Karrax? This might be our only chance." Mion lifted Jamie and pushed his way through the dark figures, none of whom seemed to care that they were being thrust aside. They came quickly to where the Skoddermen held the cage. Jamie glanced at the robes of those at the rear and his heart sank. "He's not there, Mion!" he cried. "Wait, he's at the front. They must have changed positions."

Jamie squeezed forward and slipped a hand into the Skodderman's pocket. His fingers closed about the little bottle of antidote and withdrew quickly. The Skodderman must have felt something for he turned his hooded head. Jamie tried not to look into its dark depths. He held the bottle in his fist behind his back, silently daring the Skodderman to come and get it as he slowly edged away. High above, the dragons' cry faded and the Skoddermen fell once more under Malvolia's control, reassembling into their marching formation. The Skoddermen with the cage set off once more.

"I got it, Mion!" Jamie whispered. "How much further do you think it is to Heart's Hill?"

Mion lifted Jamie and placed him on his shoulders.

"She drives them harder than ever, Jamie," said Mion, as the army of Skoddermen broke into a run. "This swift pace will see us at Heart's Hill a little before sunset."

"Won't you get tired?" Jamie said, genuinely concerned.

"Do you wish me to be tired, Jamie?" Mion asked.

"Never," Jamie said firmly.

"Then, so be it," came the reply.

Through spinney and wood, over field and fold, the Skoddermen never slackened their pace. Jamie wondered how much longer their stamina would hold. Under the dark robes they were only flesh and blood, but he had not seen them show any desire for rest or water. The ones who carried Malvolia must have been the weariest of all, and yet they maintained their lead.

Past midday and long into the afternoon they ran, silent and relentless. Mion kept pace, following only a few strides behind Karrax.

Jamie narrowed his eyes and stared ahead into the distance. The ground was beginning to level out and the earth seemed firmer under the Skoddermen's pounding feet.

And suddenly there it was, in the blue-green distance: Heart's Hill. A great mound with a razed summit on which a stone-arched building stood. There were figures ranged about the Hill and, on its upper slopes the host of dragons that had passed them earlier. Sighting the occupied Hill, Malvolia ordered the Skoddermen to stop.

"We're there," Jamie said.

"Almost home, Jamie," Mion said without taking his eyes from Heart's Hill. Though Jamie could not see it, Mion's eyes grew misty.

"'Where first we saw Thee, last we know Thee, when Thou comest to know Thyself,'" Mion chanted. "It is an old prophecy, written on the stones themselves, long since faded while we waited for you to return, Starchild."

Jamie sighed. In spite of Jamie's expressed wish,

Mion had lapsed into calling him the Starchild again.

"Why?" Jamie asked, voicing the unspoken thought.

"Why what, Starchild?" Mion said. "What is it you wish to know?"

"Why do you think I'm the Starchild?" Jamie murmured, weary and sore. Mion pressed his hand to his heart.

"We felt you come back. We— "

But the explanation Mion was about to offer was cut short as the crowd of Skoddermen parted and Malvolia was carried through. There was an ugly expression on her face.

"It seems we are faced with a welcome committee," she said. "Do they really think that a few fire-spewing, overgrown bats, and a handful of freaks can stop me?"

"At least they'll try," said Jamie.

"Witch, let there be no blood shed on this ground," Mion said. "Let not the house of the Starchild be despoiled in anger and hatred."

"Tell him to shut his mouth," Malvolia warned Jamie. "Before I shut it for him, permanently. If that rabble had seen sense and let me have what I came for, then there wouldn't be any need to dirty your precious Henge. But will they? No, no, they want to be courageous and dead, rather than sensible and alive. Well, so be it. It matters not either way to me. Now, move. I want to get within striking distance before the light goes."

She disappeared and again the company pressed on at an easier pace now. For a while longer they trudged, until Malvolia called a final halt. Her sharp eyes had picked out bowmen on the hillside and she had stopped just out of bow-shot. Slowly, at Malvolia's bidding, the Skoddermen (apart from the four who still held the cage with Karrax in it) began to prepare themselves for battle.

Six long lines they formed, one behind the other. Most drew their long knives or swung their clubs, while those that had no weapons clenched and unclenched their long fingers.

Jamie assumed that the Skoddermen would now simply charge and hack and claw their way through the guard of Heart's Hill. Malvolia had other ideas though. She wasn't going to waste her army in a thoughtless and wild dash.

First she intended to reduce the number of her enemies.

23

The Battle of Heart's Hill

At Edwyn's insistence, Mrs Mercer and Fern mounted Timbar, and Pinch was told to board Rima. The Keeper kicked up a fuss about that. He wanted to stay on the slope of the Hill and fight with the rest of them if need be, not skulk about in the protection of the Henge. Edwyn was adamant.

"Nay, Keeper," he said. "If evil chance writes our doom, then the Star-kin must be preserved. Timbar will take them to safety, and you must be their guide and accompany them on Rima; there is none other among us knows this land so well. Stay, I bid you, for they may yet need the wisdom of your years."

Pinch was disgusted at first to think that he had nothing to offer by way of fighting, but he saw the sense in what Edwyn said.

"You are no longer Keeper of the Copse and Boscage Abouts," Edwyn said, "but the Friend and Servant to the Star-kin. Doubtless the boy Jamie is safe and well in the care of the Moargelingas by now. He is the rightful heir to Mittakar and, choose which way today ends, whether good or ill, the Starchild must be found and reunited with his kindred, that they may seek to regain what is rightfully theirs." Pinch nodded and swore that he would do all in his power to see that it would be so. Edwyn turned to Mrs Mercer and Fern.

"Such a short time have we known each other, Star-kin," he said. "And I pray that this is not the last time we will speak, but . . . "

Fern bit her lip because she thought she was going to cry, and Mrs Mercer touched a finger to the corner of her eye to wipe away a grain of dust. The Chilldrakes, who had stayed with Mrs Mercer all along, sensed her emotions for they krooed softly.

"But if I should fall here in the Battle of Heart's Hill, then at least keep the memory of me in your own hearts. The strength of my arm and the bite of my bow, such as they may prove, are ever yours to command."

"Thank you, Edwyn," said Mrs Mercer.

"Go get her," said Fern, sniffing as Edwyn turned on his heel and left the Henge.

Huge as they were, the dragons were dwarfed by the great sarcens towering over them. In the soft evening light the stones seemed like tall, silent giants themselves, sleeping as they stood.

"It reminds me of something," Fern thought, and she was all for scrambling down from her dragon's back for a closer look.

"Stay on!" said Pinch, trying to stare through one of the openings in the stone ring.

They waited in silence. Fern could feel the fires rumbling in the bellies of the beasts. The dragons showed no emotion, only their red eyes shone a little brighter.

"Oh, please let it end all right, the way it should," Fern prayed. It wasn't just the Skoddermen that threatened. Fern guessed that the dragons could handle any number of them providing they were spurred into action.

It was Malvolia herself who was the greatest danger. There was no knowing what she might do. Fern steeled herself and wondered if the strange, prickling sensation all down her back was the same feeling that Buzz Beddows felt in times of danger.

"Don't be a dimmo, Fern Mercer," she told herself. "This isn't some silly cartoon you're watching. This is real. In a few hours we could all be dead."

A wind blew through the stone ring, moaning as it passed under the archways. Once there had been writing on the faces of the stones, but the wind and the rain had long since eroded all but the faintest traces of the unknown carvers' handiwork. Fern could only guess how old Heart's Henge must be and she stared about her, half fearful that there might be the old spirits of the builders lurking somewhere in the shadows of the cold stones. It seemed that kind of place, a spot that was half-alive with memories and old magic and ghosts.

Timbar tensed beneath her and she could feel waves of uneasy thought waft through her mind.

Then there was Mack, Fern thought. Where was he right now? Was he really and truly going to come and stand here in the Henge and break the Heart so that all its power would be his? She thought of him, elderly and smiling and kind, as he had stood in the parlour in Stubbs Terrace, and then she thought of the face that she had seen in the surface of the Wurmpool.

"Please, please," she whispered aloud to the towering stones. "Please don't let Mack be a baddie." Then her thoughts turned to the battle beyond the Henge.

Down on the plain at the western slope of Heart's Hill, Malvolia's eyes narrowed to dark crescents as she stood behind the ranks of Skoddermen. She raised her hands and uttered harsh words, words of a black and malicious magic. There was a movement between the fingers of her raised hands and a snake, small and deadly, fell to the ground. Then another, identical in every detail, dropped by its side. The two snakes grew in length until they were as long as a man's arm when they split in two, the four halves forming new heads, growing and dividing so that there were eight snakes writhing at Malvolia's feet, then sixteen, thirty-two, sixty-four and so on until the witch stood on a living carpet of snakes.

"Go, dark beauties," she hissed. "Destroy them!" And one by one the snakes slithered through the feet of the Skoddermen towards the Hill.

The trolls saw the poisonous tide flow along the plain. They smiled to themselves, motioning those behind them to stand well clear. As the first of the serpents came near it raised its head, bared its fangs and struck at the heel of a troll, seeking to pierce the flesh and inject its venom. Its fangs snapped on the tough skin, the poison dribbling back into its own throat.

From the safety of her Skoddermen Malvolia leered and grinned, seeing the figures leap and swing their crude axes. Then she frowned. The snakes she had created possessed a powerful poison. Her enemies should be dying in a mass, not hopping about in some grotesque dance. Then she realised. The trolls were unaffected by the snakes and were trampling the serpents underfoot or crushing them with their axes. And, although the numbers of snakes were so great that some did manage to slip through and deal death, it was not long before Malvolia's first wave of attack was defeated. A small cheer of victory went up from the occupants of the Hill and carried to her ears on the wind. Malvolia brooded upon her next move.

Jamie glanced at Malvolia, preoccupied with her evil

thoughts, and whispered to Mion to take him to Karrax. It might be the only chance he would have to give the Chilldrake the antidote. Four Skoddermen still carried the cage on their shoulders, while a fifth stood guard. All were motionless as statues, held frozen as Malvolia dredged more black spells to destroy her enemies.

Mion lifted Jamie from his shoulders and, warily, they approached the cage. The Skoddermen made no move, bound by Malvolia's will only to stand and wait until called.

Jamie whipped the stopper from the vial of antidote and was about to push his hand through the cage bars to empty the contents down Karrax's throat, when the lone Skodderman's arm came down and hit his hand hard. He cried out and the bottle fell, rolling away over the rocky ground, spilling most of the contents. Mion jumped forward and dragged Jamie away to save him from being struck again.

"Let me go, Mion," Jamie struggled. "I have to get the bottle. There might still be enough in it to— "

The Skodderman's foot rose and fell, crushing the vial to powder. He strode to the cage, ignoring Jamie's cry of anguish, thrust a hand through the bars and placed slim white fingers on the Chilldrake's head, holding them there for a moment in a gesture that Jamie had seen once before. Karrax's eyes closed and his body went limp. The Skodderman withdrew his hand.

"Mack!" Jamie whispered. "It's you!"

The Skodderman raised his hand to the darkness of his hood, where his lips would have been. He knelt down so that the dark space of the hood was on a level with Jamie's face. Jamie peered hard, trying to discern familiar features.

"Be patient, Jamie," came the returning whisper from the darkness. "Trust me."

"Never," Jamie said, staring with disbelief at the antidote that soaked into the ground. "Do you know what you've done?"

"There was only poison in the bottle," Mack said hurriedly. "It was poison that Malvolia was giving Karrax, not an antidote. She lied."

Jamie shook his head. "Why should I believe you?" he said. "You betrayed us. You stole the Heart, and now you've killed Karrax."

"He's sleeping," said the hooded Mack. "Remember how I made your mother sleep? It will draw the poison out of him. Trust me Jamie . . . trust me."

"Trust you?" Jamie said. "I can't believe you're asking that. You can see. You've broken the Heart and taken its power, and you ask me to trust you?"

"The Heart is safe," Mack said. "I need it for only a little while longer. Do not betray me to Malvolia, Jamie Mercer. I am here to ensure that the Starchild receives his inheritance."

Mack turned his hooded face to Mion and spoke softly. *"N'damakh, Moargel. N'damakh nymroth Essillar."*

Mion listened and bowed his head. "Trust him, Starchild," he said quietly. "The blind one works now for the greatest good of all."

Jamie shook his head. He refused to believe that Mack's breaking the Heart and claiming its power would be anything but catastrophic.

"Leave me now," Mack said quickly. "She must not see you talking to me."

Mion pulled Jamie away from the cage. The thought that Mack was there with them and about to use the Heart filled Jamie with despair. Despite Mion's assurance that he meant no harm, could he believe Mack when he said that there had only been poison in the smashed bottle? By knocking it from his hands had Mack saved Karrax's life?

Ignorant of Jamie and Mack's reunion, Malvolia touched a finger to her lips in deep thought. She bent down and clawed a handful of sandy earth which she flung into the air, crying more black spells. The grains of earth hung, spinning to the rhythm of her chant, and expanding into a lethal mass of needle-sharp hail. The least fragment was sharp enough to pierce a man to the heart. At a word from Malvolia, the cloud sped over the plain to Heart's Hill.

The trolls stood firm, knowing that they could not be harmed and did their best to shield their more vulnerable friends from this new onslaught. But the trolls could not cover them all and there were many that fell to the stinging hail, cut and bloodied, blinded or dead.

Malvolia grinned to see the numbers that dropped. But there were still too many left guarding Heart's Hill for her to be sure that her Skoddermen would be victorious. She would not unleash her own formidable fire as yet. Believing the Heart to be still in the Henge, she dared not risk it being borne away on the back of a dragon simply because she revealed her own might too soon. As she stood and pondered, an evil plan crawled into her brain, and lodged there.

With a single thought she sent five of the six lines of Skoddermen advancing to the Hill, slowly at first and then in a run that brought them swiftly to within bowshot of her enemies. The Skoddermen wailed and roared as they crashed into the line of trolls who swung their stone axes. From the upper slopes of the hill spears sang and arrows whistled, most finding a mark. As the two armies clashed and fell to hand-to-hand fighting, Malvolia snapped her fingers and released the Skoddermen from her control. Then she watched.

Without her black will to guide them, the Skoddermen fell into confusion. They acted as if they were waking from a bad dream, and their simple minds could not understand why they were being set upon, and so far from their natural homes. They tried their best to defend themselves against the Mithacans, and some even managed to break away and run back along the plain, scattering in their flight.

The majority of the Skoddermen, weak and purposeless, were little match for the desperate Mithacans. Sensing that victory was theirs, they redoubled their efforts, striking with renewed energy even at those Skoddermen who had dropped their weapons and were trying to surrender. It was Edwyn who sensed that the battle was fast becoming a massacre. Above the tumult of the fighting he managed to shout loud enough to be heard by those nearest to him.

"Stay, Mittakari!" he cried. "No more killing! This battle is ours!"

The Borderers raised the cry to disengage as the Skoddermen shuffled and cowered into terrified groups. The Mithacans cried with one victorious voice while Malvolia turned to Jamie and grinned. Her plan had worked.

"But you've lost," Jamie said, hardly able to believe that the battle was so soon over and unable to understand why Malvolia should look so smug and satisfied.

"So it would appear," said Malvolia, and then she squealed with laughter.

Malvolia took from a pocket a sheet of crumpled

paper and the pen with the plastic, bobbing gargoyle. She scribbled furiously and thrust the paper to the nearest Skodderman.

"Get to the Henge," she hissed, "and give this to whoever claims to be in charge. Wait for their answer."

The Skodderman bowed his head and shuffled away. Malvolia faced Jamie.

"You see," she said. "Their new queen can be merciful. I ought, by rights, to rip them apart. But I have given them the chance to surrender . . . "

"They surrender?" Jamie said. "But it's you who've lost. Your army is crushed . . . "

"That dull-witted mess of rags and bones?" Malvolia said. "You think that was an army? They served their purpose, I suppose, and may yet again . . . " Malvolia murmured, watching the single Skodderman cross the plain, waving the sheet of paper like a white flag.

"It is a ruse," said Mion, his eyes too on Heart's Henge and his voice cold and emotionless. "She is afraid that the Heart will be removed and taken to a place of safety. She sent the Skoddermen to their certain deaths to lull the Mithacans into a false sense of security. They now presume that she is offering to surrender, but she is not. Now she threatens them anew, twofold. Firstly, though some have fled and some have been slain, the numbers of Skoddermen on the Hill still exceed the numbers of the Mithacans, who were merciful enough to spare their enemies when they saw them apparently defeated. Even though the Skoddermen are for the moment cowed, they may be brought under her control in a second with but a thought, and ordered to kill again. The witch was sure that the Mithacans would not slay thoughtlessly in cold blood. Thus she has worked her force into the Mithacan camp."

Malvolia stared at Mion with something like admiration in her dark eyes.

"You know, the fool has some brains after all," she remarked.

"You said a twofold threat, Mion," Jamie whispered.

Mion looked sad. "She now threatens to destroy you. She places a terrible choice upon them. Either they render up the Heart, or she kills you."

"Nice touch, don't you think?" said Malvolia.

"Then she might as well do it now," Jamie cried. "Because they'll never give up the Heart. Never." And he smiled at Malvolia to show that he was not afraid.

"Well, my little hostage," Malvolia sneered. "I suggest we see what happens when we get to the Henge."

"Thus the Starchild shall return to where he began," said Mion, resuming his unfocused gaze upon Heart's Hill.

"Oh, it's Starchild again, is it?" Malvolia nearly spat out the words. "Just when I was thinking you had potential."

Her eyes suddenly fell on the cage and the still form of Karrax.

"Ah. It's dead then?" she whined in mock pity.

"Yes . . . " Jamie said. "I . . . I stole the antidote from the Skodderman and gave it to Karrax, but it was too late."

Malvolia laughed obscenely. "I *knew* you would!" she cried. "Don't you know that you've killed him, you little fool? There was no antidote, there never was. You gave him the rest of the poison that was keeping him half-dead. You killed your little Chilldrake. *You* finished him off." Malvolia drew a sharp breath. "Still, the lizard had a quick death at the end. Which is more than I can say for you, Starbrat, whatever their answer!"

How long they had waited as the battle raged, Fern couldn't say. The sun rode down the sky and the air grew colder with the approach of evening. Despite Edwyn's order Pinch dismounted from Rima and went to peer through one of the archways in the Henge, watching the battle. It was from Pinch's commentary that Mrs Mercer and Fern learned the outcome of the Battle of Heart's Hill and of the apparent defeat of Malvolia. Fern's first thought when she heard that the battle was over was for Edwyn.

"Is he hurt?" she called. "Edwyn, I mean."

"Takes more than a few finger-snicking Skodderrags to bodge a Borderer. Edwyn has the Skodderslutch under guard," he called from the gathering gloom of the archway. There was a note of disappointment and puzzlement in his voice as he muttered, "Funny. Wasn't much of a set-to-do, after all, 'septing for those stoney shard-edges; they felled more than a few of us. Hello?"

"What, Pinch?" Mrs Mercer asked. "What is it?"

"Skodderbod," Pinch replied. "Trampsing toward the Hill, waving a white flagget."

"Then it's over," Mrs Mercer breathed. "Malvolia has surrendered. Can you see her, Pinch?"

"No," said the Keeper. "Last time I caught a gleam of that one was when she threw the pointy dust at us. Then she flobbed back down a dummock. Oh . . . 'tain't a flagget, Looey Smurser. It's a message. Edwyn's a-fetchin' it."

Pinch stepped back into the Henge and a moment later Edwyn clattered in on a borrowed horse.

"She has sent this," he said, springing down. Pinch took the paper, screwed up his eyes and read:

"'What make is your hiffy? Tick box if shown or state other,'" Pinch frowned. "This is some dark spell I'll be bound. Rima, burn it quickly before— "

"Wait!" Mrs Mercer cried, remembering suddenly, just as Pinch held the sheet down for Rima to light. "That's a page from her clipboard, the one she was asking me questions from. It's not hiffy, it's hi-fi, Pinch. There must be something on the back of the page."

Pinch flipped the sheet over and read again.

"You will give me what I came for and you will surrender it to me now. You will acknowledge me as your rightful queen and you will kneel before me when I claim the power that is mine. You will do this and you will do it now. I have the boy. I have the Starchild. At present he lives. For how long he lives is for you to decide."

Pinch let the page droop.

"She's got Jamie?" Fern said, horrified. Mrs Mercer's blood ran cold.

"Fern," she said, "I thought you said that he was all right."

"But he *was*, Mum," Fern protested. "I promise he was. Jamie must've been captured after Timbar let me look into Wurmpool. I don't know how. Edwyn, what do we do now?"

"Edwyn would do only what I'm going to do. Leastways I hope so," said Pinch grimly. "Rest easy, Looey Smurser, we ain't about to do the dirt on the kidling. Look at it this way. The Heart isn't here but Malvalvohag don't know that. If we let her into the Henge, then at least we've got her where we want her, as it were, with Jamie, and away from whatever twitching Skoddermen she's kept in reserve. Them gangling bone-bags can be dealt with by the others if there's any trouble."

Mrs Mercer sighed with relief as Edwyn nodded his silent approval of Pinch's decision.

"Your reasoning is sound," said Edwyn. "It is a good plan."

"S'only one I've got," said Pinch. "Now, be so good as to tell the Skodderfilth to take back this message, eh, Master Edwyn. Tell him to tell Malgarbage we agree. She can enter the Henge, if she comes without any of her traipsing traitorous crew, and if – and make this quite clear – *if* she brings both Jamie and the Childerdrag. How does that sound?"

"I do not trust the witch," said Edwyn. "The battle seemed too swiftly won. I feel the first twitch of the snare that she thinks to slip about our necks. I . . . I am torn. The Skoddermen seem beaten but— "

"Know what you mean," said Pinch. "But look at it this way, Master Edwyn. We got the Flemmings. Any funny business and they lets fly with all the hodge and roary whuff they can muster. You think she'll stick it long if'n these biddies blast her, eh? They won't let no harm come to the Star-kinder. Not when the Starbaby himself is in their sights."

"I hope you are right, Keeper," said Edwyn. "I feel duty-bound to the Star-kin, but I am also a Borderer and have taken an oath to protect my people. I would not have them caught unawares."

"Go, Edwyn," said Mrs Mercer. "The dragons will look after us."

Edwyn bowed his thanks and departed. Then they waited. It was getting gloomy in the Henge now, though at the western edge, where the archways let in the light of the setting sun, golden wedges of sunlight cast bright pools on the close-cropped grass.

It was at one of these bright doorways that she appeared, a black silhouette against the strong light. Malvolia Du Mal, still in the long pink coat, still with the fat smiling face of Miss Dummel, still with the same cloying scent that crept on the evening air and tickled Fern's nostrils.

She stepped forward, followed by Jamie who was holding Mion's hand. Behind Mion shuffled a Skodderman, bearing the broken and seemingly lifeless Karrax. The Chilldrakes whirred and fretted, their small bodies trembling with anger and sorrow.

"I said none of your filth in this place!" Pinch cried.

Malvolia, some forty or so feet away, smiled. "I needed him to carry the lizard," she said. "Besides, what harm can one Skodderman do? He hasn't even got a knife."

"Jamie?" Mrs Mercer called. "Are you all right? She hasn't . . . ?"

"I'm fine, Mum," Jamie said. He tried to move forward but Malvolia laid a fat hand on his shoulder, digging in with her nails. Mion stared around the Henge like a tourist in a cathedral.

"Where is it, then?" Malvolia cried, her cold voice ringing around the stones of the Henge. "Where is the Heart?"

"It's where it's always been," Pinch lied, pointing to the stone casket in the centre of the Henge. "In Heart's Ease. Where it will always be, if I've got any say in the matter."

Malvolia laughed, loud and long. "Well now," she cried. "We shall just have to see about that, won't we?"

24

Malvolia

Malvolia's leering, triumphant pride was awful to see, as she stood at the centre of Heart's Henge. She pressed her fingers lightly to the bridge of her nose. Down on the slopes of Heart's Hill the Skoddermen, their simple minds enslaved and bound again to Malvolia's domineering and dark thoughts, roused themselves with one cry and attacked the Mithacans again with a renewed fury.

Malvolia smiled, hearing the shouts and clamour of renewed battle.

"That is so we are not disturbed," she explained. Then, ignoring the great dragons, who followed her steps with icy stares, she walked purposefully over to the stone casket, Heart's Ease, and grasped the lid. With as much effort as she would use to lift a cushion, she flipped the weighty stone and sent it crashing to the ground, where it smashed in two. She bent over and gazed into the depths of the exposed casket. For a moment she froze, and then she lifted her head. Fern could have whooped for joy, seeing the bewilderment flicker in Malvolia's eyes.

"Where is it?" she murmured. "Which one of you removed it?"

"Is is not there?" Pinch asked innocently. "Why then,

Malvollytrash, I'm afraid that you've had a wasted visit. Tush, tush, well maybe next time, eh?"

Pinch's taunting roused Malvolia's anger.

"Don't trifle with me, slug!" she bellowed. She raised an arm and pointed at Jamie. The beginnings of white fire crackled at her fingertips. "Bring me the Heart, and bring it now, or he dies!"

The dragons stirred. Fern laid a hand on Timbar's brow. "Now!" she thought. "Burn her to ash." Timbar shifted uneasily, but his great beak remained steadfastly closed.

Without a word, without a glance at anyone save Malvolia, Mrs Mercer slid to the ground from Rima's back.

"So," said Malvolia, holding out one hand and keeping the other pointed at Jamie. "You have it. You who haven't even a dishwasher. Bring it over, slowly. And no tricks, unless you want to see your spawn roasted alive where he stands."

"Mum?" Fern said, but Mrs Mercer ignored her, and walked over to face Malvolia. The fingers of the witch's open hand started to twitch greedily.

"Give it to me, now!" she hissed.

"Oh, I will," said Mrs Mercer, taking a deep breath. "I'll give it to you good and proper, you devil's bitch!" And she swung her closed fist with all the might she could, smack into Malvolia's nose and mouth.

Malvolia staggered back, throwing her hand to her face, tasting her own blood. Her eyes were like pools of red fire as she steadied herself. No one, no one had ever dared to strike her before. And no one would ever do so again. With a scream of pain and hate, she sent a blast of wild power that caught Mrs Mercer full in the chest. It threw her backwards with its force, lifting her like an old doll, and flung her at the feet of Rima, where she lay motionless.

Jamie knew what his mother had done. Aware that the dragons would not attack unless an enemy struck the first blow, Mrs Mercer had deliberately provoked Malvolia into action, and sacrificed her own life to spare the others.

Fern was sobbing and calling out, begging her mother to get up, but there was no response. Mrs Mercer didn't move.

"You black-souled, heartless hag!" Pinch cried, waving his fist. Spurred to action by Malvolia's open attack upon one of the Star-kin, Rima reared, opened his beak and belched yellow fire directly at Malvolia. The flames engulfed the witch and the pink coat instantly caught light. Timbar roared and clawed at the air, nearly throwing Fern from his back, adding his own fire to Rima's conflagration. Jamie threw up his arms against the fierce heat and light and he could just make out the black, dumpy shape of Malvolia wavering in the midst of the roaring white heat, heat that Pinch had said could melt rock itself. For three long minutes the dragons flamed, their release of fire acting as a trigger to the dragons on the hillside. They too sent their own flames scorching into the ranks of warring Skoddermen, igniting their dark robes and illuminating the fight. Timbar and Rima flamed until their furnaces were empty and their fires were dead.

And it had no effect whatsoever. Malvolia, her pink coat burned away, stood robed in black cloth, untouched by the flames. Behind the harmless fire she had started to stretch, stretch as she had done in the parlour at Stubbs Terrace, and now she stood, as proud and tall and terrible as the standing stones that surrounded her. She threw back her head and laughed into the evening sky, and when she turned to stare at her enemies her face was as dark as the lowering clouds behind her.

"Did you really think that Wurmfire could hurt me?" she hissed at Pinch. She mocked Jamie. "I said that nothing, *nothing* in this world could harm me. Do you think I am a fool? Now, where is the Heart? Speak! The brats will be next to feel my wrath."

She raised a mighty hand to dash Fern from the spent and weary Timbar's back when Pinch's voice rang out clear and cold.

"You are too late, Malvolia. We don't have the Heart. The gloomling has it."

Malvolia creased her huge brow and stayed her hand.

"What are you saying, insect?" she bellowed. "Gloomling?"

"He means Mack." said Jamie, fighting back tears. "You said you wanted answers to your questions; well, here they are. Mack did come with us. We used the Heart to get here. You called my mum stupid . . . but it's you who's stupid. Stupid, stupid, stupid! Mum had the Heart all the time, way back in Stubbs Terrace. She used it to come here and stop you too. And do you know what? Mack came with us. Mack! Caspar McGee. He came with us with the same greed for power that you have. *He's* got the Heart, you monster." Jamie crouched and ran to where his mother lay. Mrs Mercer was cold and pale, but as Jamie held her hand and squeezed it, her eyelids fluttered. Fearful lest Malvolia should notice Jamie went on, "You could have had it the day you called at our house, if only you'd known. Karrax gave the Heart to Mum when she was a little girl, and Mum kept it. She kept it and forgot what it was, and leaving it with Mum was the best hiding place of all, because nobody would think that such a treasure was hidden in a scruffy little house in a scruffy little street. Evil people like you who think you're so clever aren't clever at all. You're all just – just dimmos."

Malvolia wailed, realising the extent of her own folly.

"The gloomling?" she howled. "McGee? McGee has the Heart of Mithaca?"

"You were after Karrax," Jamie cried. "You knew he couldn't help skipping between worlds, just for the fun of it, and you learned to follow his tracks. But what you didn't know was that Karrax had smelled you too. He knew you were after him and that you might at some time stumble across the Heart. So he came back for the Heart to take it to his own world where it would be safe for ever. Only you got to Karrax first . . . and he did the next best thing. He brought you here. Oh, you could do damage, Karrax knew that. But while the Heart was safe somewhere, then so was the spirit of Mithaca, and there would always be a part of it that you could never conquer, a part that could always turn round and conquer you in time. And now you'll never be Mistress of Mithaca, because Mack has the Heart . . . and, even if I knew where he was I'd never tell you. You can kill me if you like, but I'm not frightened of you any more."

Malvolia struggled with the bitter knowledge that the old blind magician might, at any moment, come striding through the standing stones, with all the power of the Heart at his command. With such power he would crush her like a rotten egg. Her only thought now was for her own safety. She had to get away, she had to return to her own world. She needed time to think. But how? She cast her baleful eyes about the stone circle.

As her eyes alighted on Karrax, the little Chilldrake stirred and made a slight noise.

"What, *not* dead?" Malvolia said, and the possibility that she could still escape fired her black heart with hope.

"Bring me the Chilldrake," she screamed to the Skodderman, who hesitated and held Karrax to him. "Did you hear me?" Malvolia screeched with impatience. She stooped her towering figure and snatched up the Chilldrake.

The poison that Malvolia had fed Karrax had weakened him, and although Mack's enforced sleep had brought him from the brink of death, Karrax was still too weak to move. Malvolia shook Karrax violently from side to side in her efforts to wake him.

Suddenly Jamie's heart was thumping. The hooded figure of the Skodderman was sidling towards him, and Jamie caught a glimpse of his shoe: Mack's shoe. *Mack* was the Skodderman who had carried the Chilldrake!

Taking advantage of Malvolia's distracted attention, Mack crept up and knelt down by Jamie.

"Mack, why don't you help us? You can save Mithaca, you can save all of us," Jamie whispered. "Use the Heart. Use it now and save us."

"I can't," Mack murmured from the hooded shadows around his face. "If I unlock the stone, I could not trust myself to use its power wisely. Oh, I would destroy Malvolia, but I could not stop myself from taking her place. I have looked into the very bottom of my soul and despised what I saw there. I was going to use the Heart for my own ends. But now, I can't even use it to save my friends. I daren't, Jamie. I only hope that one day you will understand what I did and forgive me. Now, the Heart belongs to you."

He glanced quickly to Malvolia and then placed the small Heart in Jamie's hand. "It's up to you, Jim. It's all up to you and I'm sorry. Truly, truly sorry, Starchild."

Without another word and without the borrowed sight of the surrendered Heart, Mack felt his way back to the rim of the stone circle.

Jamie clutched the Heart. Even Mack believed that he was the Starchild. Of course, he had believed it before anyone else because Essillar was one of the words he had used in the kitchen at Stubbs Terrace, when he sent Karrax away. Jamie shook his head. He was Jamie Mercer from Stubbs Terrace! He was no sorcerer, no Starchild. He was nothing. He stared at his mother's pale face and he heard Fern's awful sobs. Mum might have been able to use the Heart. She had brought them to Mithaca with it, and she could talk to Karrax, surely that was special. And Fern, Fern could hear Wurmsong; maybe even Fern could use the Heart. He could do nothing.

"Mack," Jamie cried, not caring who heard. "Mack, come back. I can't do it. I can't!"

Malvolia turned her terrible face to where Jamie knelt. "Who are you talking to?" she demanded, her dreadful anger returning. She saw Jamie's fingers close about something in his palm. Her voice rang chill and hollow.

"What have you got? What is it? I demand that you tell me!"

Jamie stood up. "I'm not afraid of you," he said. Then louder, as if he was trying to convince himself, "I'm not. I'm not afraid of you." He was holding the Heart so tightly that it was hurting his hand. As he stood in Malvolia's black shadow, tall above him, he began to tremble. At least he would try. He raised the fist that held the Heart and he cried:

"Go away! Go to Hell or somewhere. Go to anywhere that'll have you."

Malvolia dropped Karrax to the ground. "Why," she mocked. "What a sudden change. Suddenly very courageous, very brave. Kill him!" she yelled to the Skodderman at the Henge's edge. "Kill him, I command you! I want to watch him die!" Malvolia's eyes swept the stone circle and she saw that the man remained motionless. Malvolia shuddered with rage and was about to blast the wayward Skodderman when Jamie cried out: "*I've* got the Heart, Malvolia!"

On Timbar's back, Pinch pricked up his ears, and at the edge of the stone circle Mion smiled.

A deadly light was kindled in Malvolia's eyes. "But you said . . . " she began, and then she leered. She turned to the silent Skodderman.

"It's you. It is you, isn't it, McGee?"

Malvolia raised herself to her full height. The fulfilment of her dreams and desires was still just within her grasp. She frowned, huge and dark and terrible . . . and curious. She who was now within moments of unguessed power could afford to pause.

"But why didn't you use the Heart?" she mused. "No, let me guess. Couldn't bring yourself to break the Heart? Couldn't trust yourself not to give in to the greed that drove you the last time? Oh, McGee . . . " she called to the deepening night beyond the stones. "How noble and true and how utterly, utterly foolish you are. But how grateful *I* am."

Her eyes returned to Jamie. "Give it to me . . . " she said, holding out a hand that could crush him with one blow. "Give . . . it . . . to . . . me . . . now!"

Jamie had never prayed before. At church in the special end-of-term services he would bow his head while everyone else around him did the same and he would mumble some words that meant little. Now he prayed. It was just a small, silent prayer for help, and it flew from his own heart like a tiny, unseen bird, fluttering into the night.

Pinch, who was praying just as hard in his own way, said, "Run, kidling, run and save yourself!"

"Stay, Starchild!" Mion's voice rang out like a bell. "You are home and you have the Heart. There is nothing and none to fear. Child of the Stars, call upon the Stars. Receive your inheritance!"

All kinds of thoughts were crashing in Jamie's head. There was the thought that Malvolia's great hand would snap him in two at any moment. There was the thought that his mother lay on the ground behind him, needing help. There was the thought that, though he had been in Mithaca only a short time and ridden a dragon, he had not even glimpsed a fraction of the wonders that Mithaca held. There was Mion, and his glorious, ridiculous, misguided faith that he was the Starchild. There was a fleeting thought for Mack, who, in a way, *had* beaten his own greed because he had recognised his own weakness. There was even the thought, strange as it was, that unless he, Jamie Mercer, the nothing from Stubbs Terrace, came through and beat Malvolia, Fern might never see another episode of Revoltron, renegade robot from the planet Znarl. He closed his eyes, waiting for the end.

Then Jamie heard Mack and Mion's voices crying as one: *"Ach inshoras bei tahonn, bei talithon y-aldha-andhrovadh!"*

Malvolia turned her head, recognising the words that would unlock the power of the Heart.

"No!" she boomed. "Silence! Silence!" She kindled white fire in her palms to strike down Mion and Mack.

Jamie felt the Heart start to burn in his hand, as Mack and Mion chanted: *"Tuar meidar, tuar diskhelion. Tuar d'neglin Mittakar. Ish behan . . . "*

"Essillar . . . " Jamie murmured, feeling the heat from the Heart rise in his fist, and knowing in his soul what the words meant. "O hear me you who came before and whose heart I hold. You whose spirit is my spirit, whose mind is my mind. I am come again. I am strong again. I am home again. Ish behan Essillar. I *am* the Starchild."

And Time stopped.

Overhead the stars glittered cold and distant, their flickering light the only movement or sign of life. Malvolia was poised, about to strike, frozen in her fury. Mion stood, a smile on his lips, the final word of power still echoing in his ears. Fern was caught mid-sob, Pinch sat like a statue on Timbar's back, his eyes wide and staring. The Chilldrakes hung in the air, captured like butterflies, pinned to the gathering night. The dragons themselves were still and as silent as the Henge-stones, as immobile as Mrs Mercer on the ground. No one moved; no one could move.

Jamie uncurled his fingers and looked at the Heart. No longer a dull and lifeless stone but the bright gem that once graced the forehead of the first Starchild, it shone upon his palm like a star itself, flashing with a brilliant blue-white light that spoke to Jamie.

"Miharu Essillar," the light sang. "Starchild, hail!"

Jamie smiled, feeling the ancient and star-born power of the Heart flow into him, returning after countless ages to the vessel it was meant to fill. What was it that Malvolia had said? Jamie thought. Nothing in this world could harm her, that was it. And Mion, Mion had said call upon the Stars. Perhaps, yes perhaps, there was a way to defeat the witch after all.

He raised his fist again, fingers closed about the Heart, its cold light streaming from his hand.

And, as the Starchild thought, so his thoughts became reality. The blue light spun in a dance of making and building.

And Time resumed.

Malvolia's eyes blazed, but it was with the reflected light of powerful floodlights. Malvolia was stunned, mystified both by the sudden intense light and the whine of engines. Jamie sank to his knees. Pinch buried his head in his hands, terrified. Even the dragons had nothing in their long memories with which to compare this. Fern raised her tearful face and her jaw fell open. And Mion, only Mion remained unmoved, unaffected by the sight of the friendly, smiling face that winked at Jamie through the toughened glass of the cockpit of the space-cruiser *Astrogon* as it roared into the Heart's Henge, with Buzz Beddows at the controls . . .

25

Victory

Buzz Beddows, leader of the Stargang, Captain of the *Astrogon*, and arch-enemy of Revoltron, renegade robot of the planet Znarl, instantly added the looming, dark figure of Malvolia Du Mal to his long list of enemies of the Universe. He manoeuvred his space-craft into the centre of the stone circle and faced the glowering sorceress. There was a whirr (not unlike the sound of an angry Chilldrake, Jamie thought) as Buzz Beddows armed the onboard laser-cannon. His voice rolled, rich and deep out of the ship's address-unit.

"Surrender, in the name of the Inter-Galactic Law Enforcement Patrol," Buzz called.

"Itraglectic Lorforst Pothole? Whassat, podling?" Pinch breathed in Fern's ear, but Fern was too amazed to even begin to explain.

"It's him!" she said. "It's Buzz Beddows. It's the buzzboy!"

Jamie raised his eyes and stared first at the *Astrogon*, then at Malvolia, who was gaping like a stranded fish, and then he glanced at Mion, who stood with his arms folded. He could not hear what Mion said over the noise of the *Astrogon*'s engines, but in the ship's glaring lights he saw Mion's mouth form the words.

"As you wished, Starchild."

The Chilldrakes karked and flitted as the huge, sleek craft hovered over their heads. Malvolia screamed in temper and unleashed a whip of white fire. It snaked across the bows of the *Astrogon* and slithered harmlessly off into the night sky.

"This is your last chance, madam," Buzz boomed through the night. "I have never fired upon a female yet, and have no wish to do so now. Please do not give me cause."

Fern was so proud to think that her hero still had good manners, even in a moment of crisis.

"Blast her, Buzz!" Fern cried, hugging Pinch.

"Frizzle the hag!" Pinch yelled.

Malvolia tried another futile burst of energy, and swore to herself in fury. Escape would come later, first there was revenge. She saw Mrs Mercer and Jamie huddled at her feet. And she saw the spokes of light that shot from Jamie's clenched fist as the Heart of Mithaca blazed with life.

"You!" she hissed at Jamie. "This is all your doing. I could have had it all, everything!" She raised one massive foot, and was about to bring it down on Jamie and Mrs Mercer, when a warning shot of green laser-fire sang past her left ear, scorching her with its heat.

Malvolia tottered back in pain, one hand to the side of her head, and crashed into the standing stone at her back. The great sarcen quivered with the impact and swayed. Flakes and shards of stone showered down. Mion hurried forward and knelt down by Jamie and Mrs Mercer. Another crack of laser-fire spat out from the *Astrogon*'s cannon, catching Malvolia while she was still off balance. It sizzled down one side of her face and left a black scorch-mark against her pale cheek. Malvolia hauled herself upright, disturbing the standing stones even more with her weight. She screamed with frustration and pain, and raised her arms above her head. Between her splayed hands her own power forked like lightning.

"Your last chance, madam! Surrender now, or suffer the consequences!" Buzz Beddows announced with complete calm. It was hard to tell which angered Malvolia more; the soft-spoken voice that ordered her to surrender, or the green, searing energy that would hurt her if she refused.

Malvolia reached back and grasped a stone lintel. She strained and pulled, wrenching it away and swinging it like a gigantic fly-swatter.

"The Atomiser, Buzz!" Fern squealed, almost squeezing Pinch in two.

"The Attem Eyeser!" Pinch echoed at the top of his voice, his eyes nearly popping out of his head. "Whatever it is, Buzzboy, the Podling says use it!"

But Buzz Beddows' hand was already flickering over the controls. As Malvolia lifted the stone club to bring it smashing down on the *Astrogon*, a small panel opened at the front of the ship and a star-bright missile whistled forth. It struck the stone and turned it instantly into a grey powder that rained down as harmless dust, twinkling in the *Astrogon*'s floodlights.

Malvolia thrashed and clawed at the air and was rewarded with a laser-bolt across her other cheek. She wheeled, intent now on destroying anything and everything in her blind hatred and hurt. She sent an arm smashing into the roofless arch at her back, dislodging a thousand years of settlement and patient stone guard with one blow. The stone rocked on its foundations and then, like a massive domino, it fell against its neighbour, jarring that from its place. Once, twice more, Malvolia pounded the stones, heedless of the damage she was doing to her own arm, so numbing was her anger.

Mion threw himself across Jamie and Mrs Mercer as chunks of stone, big as fists, fell around them. The standing stones creaked, their lintels cracked, and the whole stone circle heaved and swayed as if, at any moment, the great stones would uproot themselves and walk. Heart's Henge was ending its days, fulfilling at least one of the old legends, for the old stones were dying and in their death-dance they would crush the malice that was Malvolia Du Mal.

"We have to get away," Pinch cried above the noise of the *Astrogon*'s engines and the sickening crunch and groan of uprooting stones. "Leave Malvalvohag to the wizzling boat and the Buzzboy! Come on, Jamie . . . Looey Smurser . . . come, quickly."

Mrs Mercer, helped by Jamie and Mion, stood groggily. Mion seeing that she could hardly stand unaided, picked her up in his arms like a small child and lifted her on to Rima's back. Timbar was already beating the air, hovering a man's height from the ground, and Rima started to lift too, scattering the Chilldrakes with his tail.

"Wait, Rima, wait!" Jamie cried, rocks and stones clattering around him. Mion picked up Jamie and almost threw him on to Rima's back.

"Nothing shall harm the Starchild," he laughed, and slapped Rima on the flank. "*Geharran Fiorwerrym mei t'gerryth*!" he cried. "Go! Carry the Starchild to safety!"

"I'm not leaving you," Jamie called, trying to dismount, but Mrs Mercer clung to him, and kept him on the dragon's back. As one, Timbar and Rima spread their wings and leapt swiftly into the air. They passed below the *Astrogon* just as Buzz Beddows fired the laser cannon in a triple burst. Malvolia saw the dragons rise and tried to swat them like flies with her great fists. She would have used her own fire to bring them down too, but every time she raised her arms the cannon on the *Astrogon* spat a slicing line of green light that scored across her hands.

Malvolia was losing the fight, and she was losing it badly. There seemed nothing she could do to stop the stinging and the singeing that she was getting from the *Astrogon*. She even tried to use her own bulk to drag Buzz Beddows out of the sky, but the captain of the *Astrogon* was too good a pilot and too used to Revoltron's tricks to be caught that way. The *Astrogon* zipped about the crumbling, shattering Henge, skimming out of the way of Malvolia's clutching and grasping arms, and dodging the falling sarcens.

Malvolia saw the dragons sweep through the air, out of the reach of her burned and bloodied hands, and she cursed as her dream of limitless power and dominion sped into the night.

Suddenly a horse and rider leapt among the teetering stones, and raced between her legs. The rider, her long golden hair streaming with the wind of her ride, sped across what was left of the grassy circle within the stones, bent slightly in the saddle, and threw a strong arm about Mion, hauling him up on to the horse behind her.

With a cry of, "One for the Borderers!" Licia spurred her horse and drove it between a collapsing arch, a fraction of a second before it crashed down. High in the night sky on Rima, Jamie saw the rescue and he wept with joy.

Heart's Hill was ablaze with the green light of the laser cannon, and the periodic flares of white fire from

Malvolia. The dragons flew on and Jamie heard Fern give a sudden, great yell of joy.

"He's got her in the energy-net. Look, look, Pinch. He's got her! It's just like the real thing. I mean, it *is* the real thing. Look, oh Timbar, stop please. We're safe enough now and I have to see. Pinch, you have to watch this."

Timbar slowed, judging that they were at a safe enough distance from the crumbling Henge and the danger of the battle that still raged. As his own dragon's speed dropped Jamie glanced behind to see what Fern was yelling about.

From the undercarriage of the *Astrogon* Buzz had released a lattice of sizzling blue energy that ensnared Malvolia, hauling her off her feet. She tore at the web with her claws, and gnashed at it with her teeth. She tried to cut it with lashes of white fire, but nothing that she could do would make it give or break. In an effort to wriggle through the holes in the net Malvolia snapped shut like a rubber band, into the familiar dumpy shape of Miss Dummel. The energy net shrank with her, and when she stretched in an effort to snap her bonds, the net grew about her like a second skin. She writhed and twisted and cursed, and shot indiscriminate bolts of white fire.

Sure that the net would hold, whatever size Malvolia took, Buzz fired the engines into overdrive, and the *Astrogon* soared into the starlit sky. Malvolia's curses subsided into frustrated and futile pleading. Timbar and Rima hovered, letting their riders stare after the *Astrogon* and its tearful, beaten baggage, until the light of the engines and the blue glow of the energy-net were no bigger than the pinpoints of distant stars.

Malvolia Du Mal was gone.

And it was then, in the silence of their triumph, that Jamie remembered Karrax. In their haste to escape, they had left the little Chilldrake on the ground where Malvolia had dropped him. Jamie stared at the black silhouette of Heart's Hill and the ruins of Heart's Henge.

A snowflake drifted out of the sky and landed on his cheek where it melted like a tear-drop. Jamie looked about. The Chilldrakes had followed their cousins out of the ruin and there, dangling between Gidwen's and Ralawn's beaks, was Karrax, his blue eyes flashing like sapphires.

Each silently whispering their own prayer of thanks and deliverance, Fern, Mrs Mercer, Pinch and Jamie descended on the dragons' backs to the quiet slopes of Heart's Hill. All the other dragons were still there, though without a great many of their riders, who had dismounted either to guard the few Skoddermen who were left alive, or to flee themselves from the terrible destruction and noise that had gone on above them on the crown of Heart's Hill.

"I can't believe she's gone," said Jamie. "Truly gone."

"But gone where?" Pinch asked, his head in a whirl after what he had seen.

"The Prison Planet, I dare say," said Fern, exercising her special knowledge of such matters. "Along with all the other rubbish and swine that Buzz has to deal with. It's in the fifth quadrant and light years from *anywhere*, so she won't ever be back."

There was only one thought in Jamie's mind at that moment. He stared into the darkness and strained his ears until he heard the steady canter of horses' hoofs. Edwyn and Licia reined in, and Mion and Jamie exchanged glances that spoke more eloquently than words.

"We were not taken completely by surprise when the witch turned her Skoddermen upon us again," said Edwyn. "Though we were occupied a little longer than we should have liked. My heart sickened when I saw the flames and white fire leap from the stones. And when the Henge itself began to fall . . . "

"He sent me to render what help I could," said Licia, helping Mion down from her horse. "'Tis a pity I could not have used my bow. Had I come sooner . . . "

"You came just at the right time, Licia," said Jamie, running to embrace Mion.

Of course, everyone had their own stories to tell then, and they all tried to tell them at once, until Pinch, wobbling to stand on Timbar's head, called for silence.

"Hey, hey," he cried, with a hopeful note in his voice. "Afore the talking and chitterin' starts . . . anyone think to bring any grubbage?"

Edwyn had dried meat in his saddlebag and a flagon of black beer, and together, by a campfire at the foot of Heart's Hill, they told their separate tales well into the night, laughing or crying together, and everyone said how wonderful, or how brave they all thought the other was, or how clever.

Then Master Gollin Carver arrived, a little battered and scuffed, but safe. His tally of the dead and the wounded silenced everyone, until Licia braided her long hair, and sang a slow, sweet song of praise for the fallen.

Her song touched the hearts of all there and carried over the field of battle and even reached the ears of the other Mithacans, huddled in their various groups, still watching over the broken Skoddermen.

Finally, as ever, joy surfaced out of grief, and much

of the story had to be told all over again, especially the part where the Star-chariot suddenly appeared at the Starchild's bidding. Only one thing was not spoken of and that was Jamie's dream of the slain Murglings. That needn't be told he thought, not ever.

And then, of course, there were the inevitable questions: "Well, well, are you really a stodging Murgling?" or "What else did you see in Wurmpool, Ferny?" or "How did you feel when Malvolia blasted you, Mum? Did your whole life flash in front of your eyes like they say?" or "Poor Mack. I wonder what he'll do now?" and so on, until one by one they fell asleep beneath the stars until only Jamie and Mion were left awake.

"You are not tired, Starchild?" Mion asked.

"I thought I told you to call me Jamie," Jamie laughed gently. He was tired, very tired, but he couldn't sleep. "I really *am* the Starchild, aren't I, Mion?" he asked, staring up at the starry sky.

In answer Mion lifted the pendant and chain that he wore and placed it about Jamie's neck.

"I – don't you want this?" he said. Mion shook his head.

"I wore it to remind me. Now I shall never forget. Keep it, Jamie Mercer; it becomes you well and will serve as a carrier for the Heart. Why do you seem sad? Has not all happened to the Starchild's satisfaction?"

"It's nothing," Jamie said. "I was just thinking of the Henge. It was rather beautiful in an old, cold sort of way. And now it's broken and smashed."

Mion lay back on the soft grass and closed his eyes. "It was built to hold the Heart until the heir to the stars should claim it. Do not grieve for stones, Jamie Mercer. As for the Henge, well, the Moargelingas built it the once," he whispered. "They can build it again. If it is ever needed," Mion laughed softly. "Or if the Starchild wishes it."

Jamie looked at the pendant in the soft glow of the dying campfire. It was unmarked and unadorned now, polished on both sides like a mirror. Only the reflection of his own face stared back at him.

And the night-wind, blowing through the ruins of Heart's Henge on Heart's Hill seemed to whisper, "Essillar . . . Essillar . . . "

26

Rain-washed Streets

During the night the Mithacans had gathered their dead and the dragons had borne them away to be mourned by their loved ones and buried with all honour. The Skodder dead were piled in a mound and burned to ash by dragonfire. But it was no ignoble end, for burning was always the way that Skoddermen dealt with their fellows' remains, and to go by the way of dragonfire was an honourable passing.

In the sunlit garden at Ditching the next morning Mrs Mercer and Jamie thought that they would never stop crying and hugging Pinch. Even the gruff Keeper of the Copse and Boscage Abouts was overcome with emotion, and the Chilldrakes, who had accompanied Mrs Mercer as if it was their right, whipped up a happy, but temporary snowstorm by way of thanks. There were tears of joy, of course, because Mithaca was safe, and the Heart was safer than ever, sealed in the pendant that Mion had given Jamie and that now hung about the Starchild's neck. And they cried tears of sadness as well because, despite all arguments, Mrs Mercer felt that they had to leave.

"Don't see why, Looey Smurser," Pinch scowled, making one last effort. "Star-kin belongs in Mithaca. Only right and proper that."

Mrs Mercer smiled. "You may be right," she said. "But we have our own world too, Pinch. The children have school and their friends there, and I . . . I have Stubbsterris to look after." She saw the unhappy frown on Pinch's face. "Besides," she added, quietly so that only Pinch heard, "no one said we were leaving for ever . . . "

"What about Mack?" Fern asked. "What will happen to him? I mean, he didn't really do bad, did he? He brought the Heart back, after all, *and* he stopped Jamie from poisoning Karrax."

Pinch pursed his wrinkled mouth, and then he smiled a small smile, wistful and sad.

"McGee will go unharmed as long as he wishes to remain here. You have the word of the Keeper of the Copse and the Boscage Abouts." Pinch seemed lost in thought. "Maybe – maybe the Chillydrake will bring him back to your world if McGee ever feels the need to return."

"Or maybe we'll all come back for a holiday, if Karrax fetches us," said Fern brightly, frowning when everyone laughed.

Jamie gazed about the small garden and the bushes, dark with deep and dusty shadows in the early morning light. He liked to think Mack was there, hidden by those shadows, listening. Mion touched his shoulder.

"Essillar," he said. "The Moargelingas have brought someone who also wishes to say goodbye."

Together they stole away from the others and walked through the orchard beyond the garden. There, beneath a gnarled apple tree and flanked by Murglings, was Mack.

"We found him in the early hours," said Mion. "I

thought that you would not wish to see him wander blind or come to harm."

"No," Jamie said, "you did right, Mion. Hello, Mack."

Mack, still in the robes of a Skodderman, threw back his hood.

"Miharu, Essillar," he said quietly. "Hail, Starchild," His face was serious and sad. "You are going home?"

"Mum says we should," Jamie replied. "Will you come with us?"

Mack smiled. "I think not," he said. "At least, not yet. I am tired, old. The slow pace of life here will do me good, I think. Maudy's cottage would make an ideal retreat." Mack smiled as if to reassure Jamie that he was happy enough.

Jamie nodded and then he whispered something to Mion. Mion whispered a reply and then lifted Jamie, who took the pendant and placed it over Mack's head. Mack fingered the dull stone, his face sombre.

"It's not a test or anything like that," Jamie reassured him. "Mion says that most of the power of the Heart has passed to me, that it's in me, though I'm not sure what he means. There's just enough power left in the Heart for it to call me if . . . if Mithaca needs me, or if I want to come back here. I just thought that the power left in it might . . . well, I thought you could look after it for me. Mion says that if I wish it it's all right."

The moment Mack had touched the Heart, the hazy image of a young boy had shimmered before his eyes; a young boy with a tall white-haired man at his side. Mack gazed at Jamie and was surprised by the sudden joy and peace that he felt now that he knew he was truly forgiven.

"H'middion," he said. "Thank you."

He held out his hand and Jamie shook it gently.

"Bye, Mack," he said, and he added in the voice he used for best friends, "See you soon, maybe . . ."

Without looking back, Jamie and Mion rejoined the others.

Pinch allowed Fern to give him one last farewell kiss, and Jamie raised one hand in a simple wave to Mion. It seemed a cold and distant way to say goodbye, but Mion smiled and said nothing: he did not need to. He stepped back as Mrs Mercer, Jamie and Fern held hands. Karrax spread his wings, hovered for a moment as if deciding, and then landed on Jamie's shoulder. There was a sigh like a gentle wind through the branches and the sunny and green garden at Ditching became an early morning and still lamplit pavement, bathed in the yellow light that spilled out of shop windows.

It was raining.

Jamie felt his shoulder, but Karrax was back in his own world, in Mithaca, with Pinch and the dragons and Mion and the hundred other wonders that they had only touched upon. There were no long farewells for the little Chilldrake.

They stood for a moment, their arrival unnoticed by the few people that were about at that early hour. Jamie didn't know how many times he had walked that street but it felt different, brighter somehow, in spite of the drizzling rain. He looked up at the sign that hung over the front of the building where they were standing. It was a café, and it stood in their world at the very spot where Old Maudy's house stood in Mithaca. Its sign, which Jamie had never noticed before, read: "Mack's Snacks".

Jamie smiled to himself as they walked the rain-washed streets back to Stubbs Terrace. Mithaca would never be far away. He shivered, happier than he had ever been. There *was* just the one thing, he thought, as the rain trickled down the back of his neck.

"I wish I had an umbrella," he said.

And was it his imagination, or did a deep voice really whisper at his back, "So be it, Starchild"?